Forgotten Evidence

A Novel
By Al Macy
AlMacyAuthor.com

Chapter One

WITH MY FOREHEAD RESTING on the edge of the desk, I stared at the floor. *Could the strange new client break me out of my funk?* I sat up, took a deep breath, and slapped my cheek. *C'mon, Garrett, get a grip.*

I picked up the client's letter, handwritten in neat cursive on vintage paper, and read it once more: *I shall esteem it a favor if you will grant me a brief audience on Friday next, being the thirtieth of April, in the year of our Lord 2021, on a matter of some importance. To wit: I should like to hand over an envelope which, if you opt to accept me as a client, you will hold on my behalf and in confidence, and which you shall open pursuant only to the conditions I provide. Until then, I remain, yours sincerely, Arthur Toll.*

I put the sheet down. *Who writes like that?* I looked around the office. It matched the Gilded Age style of the letter. Goodlove and Shek—I'm the Goodlove—occupies the second floor of a Victorian building constructed in 1889. Dark paneling extends from the hardwood floors to the tin ceilings. It resembles a stuffy men's club where mustachioed British gentlemen might smoke cigars and argue about the Boxer Rebellion. A butler with an aperitif on a tray wouldn't have been out of place.

Taking advantage of a recent windfall, I'd had the Persian rug cleaned and treated to banish its musty odor. That left the scent of the sea—we were only a few blocks from Redwood Point Harbor—and the smell of woodsmoke from my office's best feature: a cast-iron fireplace. I tried to have a fire most days; the crackling soothed me. I'd added a wooden rocking chair after reading that rocking heals an injured mind.

Our new legal secretary and receptionist, Miss Ida Smaridge, knocked on the doorjamb and looked at me over the top of her wire-framed glasses. "Arthur Toll is here, Mr. Goodlove. Shall I show him in?"

"I really can't get you to call me Garrett?"

"That would not be appropriate."

"Maybe you could just try it for a few days?"

"Shall I show him in?"

Miss Smaridge—I didn't dare call her Ida—had been a legal secretary since long before I was born, something she'd mentioned a few times. I was forty-six, and she was in her eighties. Late eighties.

If steel wool came in see-through white, that's how I'd describe her hair. It covered her whole head like a wispy cloud, which was more than could be said of my own hair. I had a healthy peninsula of hair top and center, fighting the good fight against male pattern baldness. At least it was thick enough that you couldn't see bottom. Heavy creases from the sides of her nose extended down to her wrinkly jowls, and her jaw seemed to articulate open and closed independently of the rest of her face. I sometimes pictured her as a ventriloquist's dummy made from a shrunken-apple-head doll.

But Miss Smaridge was no dummy. If female lawyers had been a thing back in the 1960s—when Ruth Bader Ginsburg was rejected by many law firms despite having graduated first in her class at Columbia—Smaridge would probably have founded a big firm in New York City or San Francisco. In addition to her familiarity with the law, she had a head for detail and organization. I'd bet her favorite expression was: *A place for everything and everything in its place.*

"Mr. Goodlove?" She pulled her glasses down a bit more so she could better hit me with her disapproving rays.

"Yes. Please send him in. Thank you, Miss Smaridge." I hoped she would warm to me over time.

My doctor once told me I had "smiling depression." Like the chocolate in a Tootsie Pop, my sadness was hidden inside a hard-shell outer layer. I squared my shoulders and put on my successful-attorney game face as Arthur Toll entered my office.

The top of his head was disproportionately large, like a cartoon mad scientist with an oversized brain. The effect was amplified by his baldness, as if his head had outgrown his hair everywhere but on the sides. Despite that, I pegged his age at mid-thirties. He was only around five foot five and slim, almost anorexically so. He and I shared an advantage: We both looked smart. His intelligence was underscored by scientific degrees from Harvard, MIT, and Oxford—I'd Googled him.

Toll wore a suit and tie, way too formal for Humboldt County. Overall, he wasn't freakishly unusual, but I guessed he'd been bullied as a kid.

He bowed. "I wish to thank you for seeing me, notwithstanding my short notice and your undoubtedly hectic schedule."

I bowed back. Handshaking had died out during the COVID-19 pandemic.

I gestured to a visitor chair. "How may I help you today, Dr. Toll?"

"What a singular office you have, sir. I would like to take a further moment before we conduct our business. May I?" He swept his arm around the room.

"Certainly. I do have a wonderful office, something I often fail to appreciate." I didn't have any other appointments that morning, in part because I'd been offloading some of my cases to my partners: my wife, Jen Shek, and my daughter, Nicole Goodlove.

Toll walked over to a large photograph on the wall. It was a black-and-white shot of a huge pipeline of a wave about to crash on the tip of Redwood Point's North Jetty. The ominous sky suggested an approaching storm. The engaging feature of the photo was a pair of wheeling seagulls, contrasting sharply with the dark clouds behind them.

"What a remarkable study this is. It portrays both motion and danger simultaneously while preserving, at the same time, a pleasing balance of composition. Truly exceptional, something I can recognize despite my total lack of knowledge of photography." He started toward the chair.

"My son took that."

Toll stopped and turned back toward the photo. "Indeed! I hope he is richly rewarded for his talent, and I have confidence in presuming he is a professional photographer. Is that not true?"

"Yes, he's a freelance photographer, and he manages to make a living at it. It's impressive, actually." Toby was twenty-two and, like Nicole, the product of my first marriage, a marriage that ended when his mother was killed by a drunk driver.

Arthur Toll sat in the visitor chair and pulled an envelope from the inner pocket of his suit coat. "Well, I'm taking altogether too much of your time, Mr. Goodlove, so here is the envelope to which I referred in my letter of four days ago."

I reached across my desk and took it. The flap had been sealed with wax. I flipped it over. In the same neat cursive I'd seen in his letter, he had written, *To be opened in the event that something happens to me — Dr. Arthur Toll.*

Turning it over and examining the seal once more, I said, "To be clear, you would like me to hold on to this letter and open and read it only if … something happens to you?"

"Quite so. Is that not a request you receive from time to time in your profession as an attorney?"

"To be honest, no. I've seen it happen in movies and television shows, but this is the first time I've gotten such a request." I put the letter down and took out my legal pad. "Do you feel that you are in danger, Dr. Toll?"

"I … please call me Arthur. I'd prefer to not disclose that information, and I apologize for my reticence."

"If you do feel that you are in danger, or someone else is in danger, you should be going to the police. Can you tell me at least why you want to keep this a secret, Arthur?"

He closed his eyes and chewed on his lip. He laid a few fingers on his cheek and opened his eyes. "May I say only that I am unsure of my hypotheses, and disclosing them could do great harm, or at least … no, I'd prefer to leave it at that, if I may."

"Everything you say to me will be held in the strictest confidence."

"I appreciate that, and your firm has an indubitable reputation of trustworthiness, according to my research, which I hope you will excuse, yet I've reached the conclusion that it would be advantageous, for all parties concerned, to obscure that information for now."

Despite his flowery speech, Arthur didn't have a superior air. *Why does he talk like a time traveler from another century?*

I made some notes on my legal pad. "Okay. Another issue is the phrase, 'in the event that something happens to me.' I would like to talk about the conditions under which I should open this letter. I imagine that if you, say, fell and broke your wrist, that would not be grounds for opening the letter."

He laughed. "Quite so, and you've made me realize that I should have thought this through a little more, although I can assure you I have imagined a number of circumstances under which I would wish you to open the envelope."

"Such as?"

"If I had occasion to be involved in a serious car accident which rendered me comatose, I would wish you to read the letter."

"Arthur, it's clear that you feel you're in danger. Do you think someone might want to silence you or even kill you? Is that what you're saying?"

His eyebrows jumped up, although it was no great leap of logic on my part.

"Of course," he said, "I should have foreseen that you would come to that conclusion, and I shouldn't—"

"It's the obvious conclusion. We can go together to the police. The detective sergeant at the RPPD—the Redwood Point Police Department—is a friend of mine, and her discretion can be counted on."

Arthur crossed his arms and remained silent.

I sighed. "Okay. Let's nail things down a little more. Let's say you disappear. How soon should I open the letter?"

"It is not in my nature to disappear without providing notice to my friends and colleagues or my brother, so let us say that if I have gone away with no prior notice, you should look into things, and if, at your discretion, it is warranted, you should open the letter. I can surmise your next question."

"How will I know that something has happened to you?"

"Yes, precisely." He nodded. "What do you propose? I would like to give you a retainer sufficient for you to keep tabs on me."

"Arthur, this is crazy. I—"

"I beg your forbearance in this matter, Mr. Goodlove."

"Garrett."

"Garrett. It will likely turn out that this whole matter is silly, and in a week, I'll come back here to collect the

7

letter. But I would like to cut off this line of inquiry at this time, if I may, and beg that you place your trust in my judgment for the time being."

I wasn't making any progress. "Arthur, why don't you tell me about yourself?"

"I don't wish to consume any more of your time, Garrett."

"It will help me help you if I know you better."

"That's fair," he said. "Let's see. I'm a research scientist at Vanovax, and I have a medical degree as well as a doctorate in neuropsychopharmacology, and it is the latter from which I take most benefit."

"Do you work on vaccines?"

"No. It is that for which Vanovax is famous, but they have, of late, branched out into basic research on neuropsychopharmaceuticals, and I head the small department in which we are researching whether there are any practical applications for a variant of propranolol, called propolofan, which—"

"Is that the drug that killed Michael Jackson?"

"No, although they're related. That was propofol, a drug which also has an effect on memory."

"Ah, right. Propolofan is the amnesia drug!"

Arthur laughed and ran his hand over his head. "Well, that's what the media calls it—"

"For the treatment of depression."

"No, no, no. You've been reading articles in the popular press. That application is, at the same time, speculative and far in the future. We have demonstrated only that the drug might interfere with the reconsolidation of fear conditioning through noradrenergic blockade in the amygdala of rats—sorry,

I've lapsed into jargon. Just know that the popular media, in their desire to make stories both sensational and comprehensible to the lay public, simplify and exaggerate the results of basic research."

I nodded. "Arthur, I've noticed your unusual and wonderful manner of speech. If anything, it reminds me of writers of the 1800s—maybe Charles Dickens or Herman Melville."

"Quite so, Garrett. I'm sure many people I've met have noticed my anachronistic style and yet failed to remark on it or to place its origin. I can explain it plainly: I was homeschooled as were both of my parents and, probably, my grandparents before them. Apparently, they all eschewed the progression and evolution of speaking and writing styles, something they passed down through the education of their offspring. It rarely serves me well, often leading new acquaintances to perceive me as hoity-toity, snobbish, or condescending, yet I've been unable, despite great and sustained effort, to modernize my speech. It has become an intrinsic component of my personality."

So, not a time traveler.

We continued talking, and I warmed to him. He'd received his degrees at remarkably young ages and was well compensated at Vanovax. I saw him as a great intellect who, perhaps, lacked any street sense and maybe even common sense. All the more reason to get him to present his concerns to the police.

"Arthur, as a criminal defense attorney, I see some unsavory characters, and I know that going to the police —"

He held up his hand. "May I make an observation?"

"Certainly." I wondered whether he was just trying to change the subject.

"You've been making notes on your legal pad there. What will you do with them when I leave?"

"They will go into your file. You do not need to be concerned about confidentiality."

"No, I'm not. I'd simply like to acquaint you with how it's done, or at least the way I do it, in the scientific community. I record all my observations in chronological order in a lab notebook, the pages of which are bound. That is, it's not a loose-leaf notebook. I even record my out-of-the-lab observations in that notebook. I have taken a solemn vow to record everything important that happens in my life. No pages may be removed, and my notes are taken in pen."

"You mean like a diary or a journal?"

He nodded. "Precisely. In that manner, nothing is lost or misplaced. For example, tonight I will describe not only what happened in the lab this morning, but my conversation with you. I have a good memory and should be able to document this session with significant detail. Perhaps this is a fetish of mine, but it has served me well not only in my research but in my personal life. It may not be practical in your profession, and I'm not suggesting that you change your custom, but I thought you'd be interested in that observation."

I didn't suggest that perhaps a computer app, with cross-referencing and tags, might be an improvement. I figured he was set in his ways.

We finished up the conference. Normally, I would have mailed him a summary of the meeting, but with his concern over secrecy, he didn't want that. I tried once more, without success, to impress upon him the danger of his situation.

On his way out, Arthur stopped to examine another photo. It showed my twin sister and me surfing side by side on a small but well-formed wave. Toby had snapped the photo in Brookings, Oregon, an hour and a half up the coast.

Arthur looked at the photo and then at me. "Is that you?"

"Yes. And that's my twin sister beside me."

"Remarkable. You make it seem easy. I've long had the desire to at least try surfing, yet it was my impression that the water here is too cold for the sport to be pleasurable. I see, on the other hand, that you two have wet suits on."

I'd read recently that individuals with more friends tend to be less depressed. With that in mind, I asked, "Would you like a lesson?"

Arthur frowned. "Oh, I see now that my comment could have been interpreted as angling for an invitation, but that was not my intention."

I clapped him on the shoulder. "Not at all. I'm going surfing with my daughter on Sunday, and I always enjoy seeing the sport through a newcomer's eyes."

"Thank you for that gracious invitation, but I must decline for now. I appreciate the offer."

I took a business card from my desk. "If you change your mind, just give me a call. We'd enjoy having you along, and it would give me the opportunity to show off my wonderful daughter."

He took the card and slipped it into a pants pocket.

After he'd gone, I held the envelope up to the light. It felt as if there were a few sheets of paper inside.

"Is that the letter?"

I jumped.

Coming over to the desk, my wife and law partner laughed. "You look as though I've caught you at something. Are you trying to see what the letter says?"

"Not at all." I wasn't really … but I kinda was.

Lowering her voice and affecting a British accent, she said, "So, did he speak in the same formal manner and with the same antiquated style in which he wrote?" She sat in the visitor chair and took the envelope from me.

I'd stolen Jen away from the public defender's office eight years earlier, and she'd finally agreed to become my bride in 2020. She's sixteen years my junior, which was undoubtedly the source of some of the disapproving glances I received from Miss Smaridge. Jen is an otherworldly product of a Japanese mother and Chinese father, and she always gets second looks in the courtroom—everywhere, in fact. She has delicate features and penetrating eyes that she uses to great effect when cross-examining witnesses.

She examined the wax seal and also held the envelope up to the light.

I nodded. "Arthur did speak that way, actually, although not with a British accent, if that's what you were doing. Said it's because he's from a long line of homeschoolers. He's an interesting guy and not at all snobby. Just different."

"And the conditions for opening the letter?"

"We are to open it if something happens to him."

"Really?" She put the envelope on my desk.

"Really."

"That sounds bad. Did you tell him to go to the police?"

I nodded. "Several times. I couldn't get through to him."

Her penetrating eyes bored into me.

"What?" For many years I'd found her expressions inscrutable, but I'd recently cracked the code. I'm not saying I could read her like an open book. More like the CliffsNotes version of a book. She wasn't thinking about Dr. Toll anymore; she was concerned about me.

"I'm fine," I said.

Confirming that I'd read her mind correctly, she stood, came around the desk, and pulled me up into a hug.

"Really, *koibito*, I'm fine," I said. "*Koibito*" is Japanese for "sweetheart."

She hugged me harder.

I'm a lucky man. I know it in my heart, so why does my stupid brain often think things are hopeless?

Chapter Two

LOUELLA DAVIS, GOODLOVE AND Shek's go-to private investigator, placed a box of chips in the center of the poker table. She took a pull on her e-cigar. *Almost as good as the real thing.*

Resembling The Oracle in *The Matrix*, she was a sixty-eight-year-old black woman whom no one would peg as a PI. She'd worn her kinky black hair in an Afro until joining the Los Angeles Police Department in 1974. Louella was of average height and weight and looked good for someone who'd smoked two packs a day up until her heart transplant in 2019. Her unbreakable habit wouldn't have let her anywhere near the transplant list, but when the heart of a local accident victim was approaching its Best By date, the docs had to either toss it into the trash or into Louella's chest. She'd lucked out. She kept right on smoking after the transplant, but because she limited herself to e-cigarettes with no nicotine content, her doctor gave her a reluctant okay.

On poker nights, she always selected a Cuvana e-cigar, which resembled a Cuban Montecristo, right down to the glowing flame tip. Her other constant companion: the half-frame reading glasses that hung around her neck on a beaded chain.

Most would see Louella's living room as retro, but it reminded her of the house she'd grown up in. It was crowded with overstuffed, floral-patterned armchairs as well as too many ottomans. She had to push her heavy furniture out of the way when it was her turn to host poker night, but that was no problem for her young heart.

Louella answered the doorbell with her Cuvana in the corner of her mouth. Hugging was too primal to go the way of handshakes, so she gave Jen and Nicole warm embraces. They'd Ubered over because poker night was also drinking night. Louella took their drink orders.

At twenty-six, Garrett's daughter, Nicole, was only four years younger than her stepmother. Over the summers, she'd interned at Goodlove and Shek even before heading off to Connecticut for law school, and the two women shared a close relationship. Despite growing up with a hot-tempered Latin mother—or perhaps because of it—Nicole was generally imperturbable. She'd handled the death of her mother better than Garrett, and the shared trauma had made the two close.

Nicole was cute rather than beautiful, with straight brown hair and a button nose. Perhaps because of her healthy self-esteem, she'd never, even as a teenager, felt the need to experiment with different hairstyles, try body piercings, or get a tattoo.

While Nicole was in the kitchen making sandwiches, Jen and Louella took their places at the poker table.

Louella tasted her Canadian Club on the rocks. "How's Garrett doing?"

Jen shook her head. "Not great. Surprisingly."

"I wasn't surprised," Nicole called from the kitchen. She came in holding a plate with a ham on rye in one hand and a rum and Diet Coke in the other. "I didn't predict it or anything, but I know that depression isn't as strongly related to events as people think. So I wasn't surprised that our big windfall didn't cure him."

"It made it worse," Louella said.

"Well, maybe."

"If you don't have to work hard to keep your business afloat, it gives you time to think of other things. People running away from a tiger are rarely depressed."

Jen laughed. "Did someone do a study of that?"

Nicole sat down. "Right now, on a scale of one to ten, how depressed are—ah, *shoot*, the tiger got him." She took a sip of her drink, put the glass down, and looked at Jen. "Did you tell Louella what Dad said?"

"Oh … I think that just slipped out."

"Dad rarely says things by mistake."

"Maybe it was just a joke."

"I doubt—"

"Tell me!" Louella said.

Jen and Nicole looked at each other, and Nicole nodded to her stepmom.

"Well," Jen said, "somehow we got to talking about what advice we'd give our younger selves."

"Since you guys are so old." Louella took a puff and exhaled a stream of vapor.

Jen waved the vapor away. "Do you want to hear it or not?"

"Sorry."

"So, I said I'd tell my sixteen-year-old self not to study so hard. And Nicole—"

"I said I'd tell myself to take more risks."

Louella cocked her head. "Really?"

"No one said it had to be *good* advice."

"And Garrett said?" Louella made an impatient rolling motion with her hand.

Jen took a breath. "He said, 'Kill yourself now before you have people who depend upon you.'"

Nicole gave a little headshake. "No, it was 'who love and depend on you.'"

"Whoa." Louella straightened her chips. "That doesn't sound like he was joking."

"Maybe he was just trying to liven up the discussion," Jen said.

Louella took a puff. "Or it was a cry for help."

"Yeah, I can see that."

"With some good news mixed in." Louella blew a smoke ring.

It was Nicole's turn to frown. "Good news?"

"Well … he's saying he wishes he were dead, but don't worry, 'I'm not going to kill myself, because you guys love and need me.'"

After they all pondered that, Louella shuffled the cards. "Get me drunk, and I'll tell you what he should do."

"Tell us now, Dr. Freud," Jen said.

"Did you know that Freud was usually stoned when he performed his psychoanalysis?"

Jen said, "Bullshit."

Nicole said, "That would explain the penis-envy thing."

"Well, he was a druggie. Garrett will be fine. By the way, I've already started on the Vanovax thing."

Jen and Nicole looked at each other.

"He didn't tell you? He asked me to look into the Vanovax pharmaceutical company. See if there was anything that wasn't on the up and up. Isn't that for an active case?"

Jen said, "Not really active. Kind of a potential case. Maybe he wants to get ahead of it."

"He wants to satisfy his overactive curiosity." Nicole took some macadamias from the bowl next to her poker chips.

Louella started dealing. "Doesn't matter. As I said, Garrett will be fine. Now no more serious talk—time for me to make some money off you rich-bitch ambulance chasers."

They played Texas Hold 'em, the world's most popular poker game. Each player receives two cards, then five are dealt, in stages, faceup on the table. Louella knew her opponents well. Both had studied the game extensively. Nicole had even read a book on strategy, but she tended to play too many hands, not folding enough. Jen, however, was impossible to read.

She had the best poker face. Nicole's cheeks would turn a little pink when she had a monster hand—something that was hard to fake. *Has Jen ever noticed that?* Louella's advantage was table smarts from a lifetime of weekly games with her cop friends.

She was working the long game that night, playing conservatively with low bets, preparing the ground for a good bluff. A little after eleven, Louella was dealt an ace and the king of hearts. The flop was the jack of hearts, the nine of spades, and the five of hearts. She had nothing but a flush draw and good over cards. She would be behind anyone with a pair or better. Time for a semibluff.

Jen checked, and Nicole bet three-quarters of the pot. *Was she blushing a little?* Louella added a small raise. After the turn and the river —the remaining faceup cards—had been dealt, Louella only had a pair of kings. She continued with her bluff.

All three players bet heavily, with Nicole going all in. At the final call, Jen had three of a kind. Nicole had a full house. Louella's bluff had failed. Nicole won over three hundred dollars and effectively ended the night. *Now she's definitely blushing.*

Trading in her chips, Nicole reminded Louella of her promise of advice for Garrett.

Louella freshened up her whiskey and took a sip. Savored it. "Garrett seems—"

"Did you forget something?" Jen asked. All three of them were pretty soused.

"Forget something?"

"You're supposed to say, 'I'm not a doctor, but …'"

"I'm not a doctor, but Garrett seems to be trying to fix his depression, make it go away. He should be trying to live with it. Be happy in spite of it."

Nicole scoffed. "So your cure for depression is to be happy. That makes no sense, but let's say you're right. What should he do to be happy?"

"Appreciate what he has."

"No, Louella," Jen said. "He does that. He often talks about how lucky he is. He says he knows it in his heart, but he still feels hopeless sometimes."

Louella started sorting the chips. "I saw a TED Talk called 'Hardwiring Happiness.' The guy said you have to make an effort to really pay attention to good experiences. Think about them for a minute or so, hold on to them. Let them soak in. Savor them."

She put the white chips in the box. "The brain tends to pay too much attention to negative experiences because those were important back in the caveman days. You have to consciously overcome that bias by holding on to good experiences. You have to actively appreciate your good fortune if you want to enjoy life. Or fight depression."

Both Jen and Nicole laughed.

"What?"

Nicole said, "Touchy-feely much? And you call yourself a hard-boiled PI."

Louella placed a stack of red chips into the box. "I have hidden depths."

Jen said, "Hard-boiled with a soft yolk. Back to curing depression versus being happy in spite of it. Are those two things really different? I mean, if you're happy, you don't have depression."

Louella waggled her hand, spilling a little of her drink. "Take Carly. She's deaf. You don't see her trying to hear. She—"

"No, no, no," Nicole said. "You're way off base there, Louella. First of all, there's no way Aunt Carly could hear again, and second—"

"Cochlear implants?"

"No. Those are only effective if implanted during early childhood. But second, Carly doesn't see her deafness as a disability. She has no desire to cure it. She's perfectly happy."

"Well," Louella said, "that's my point. She doesn't spend any time thinking, 'Oh, I wish I could hear.' She just leads her life. I have a feeling that every time Garrett feels down, he's thinking, *Oh, what's wrong with me? Why can't I be happy like other people?* That only makes things worse."

Jen shook her head. "I don't think it's that simple with depression. Let me rephrase—I *know* it isn't that simple. There are brain chemicals that can get out of whack and make it impossible for someone to think themselves well."

"Be glad I'm not a shrink." Louella tilted her head back, emptying her glass.

"And remember, Garrett was fine before Raquel and Patricia died," Jen said. Soon after Garrett's wife was killed, Patricia, Garrett's niece, had died during a surgical procedure.

"That was six years ago. I guess what I mean when I said you have to be happy despite your depression is you have to play the cards you're dealt in life." Louella crunched an ice cube with her teeth and closed the wooden box of chips.

Nicole fanned out her winnings and waved them. "Even if you have to bluff?"

Louella shrugged. "Something like that."

There was no way I was letting Carly drive my Tesla Model 3. My twin couldn't be a worse driver if she were a drunken monkey applying mascara behind the wheel. It wasn't any lack of ability or coordination; it was her recklessness. She viewed speed limits and traffic signs as polite suggestions. Plus, her attention tended to drift, especially when in the middle of an intense American Sign Language discussion—the kind we usually had.

After the firm's windfall settlement, I'd splurged on a top-of-the-line Tesla with all the options, including the performance package. I took great pleasure in driving it, except on those days when I took pleasure in nothing.

I was sitting in the car outside my sister's house, thinking up more similes that would describe her driving style, when she rapped a coin against my window.

After laughing at my startle response, she signed, "I want to drive." The ASL for that could almost be understood by a man on the street. The signs for "drive" and "I" are exactly what you'd expect. "Want" is signed as if grabbing something with two hands from below. In any case, I understood what she was saying. Carly was deaf from birth, and she and I had learned ASL together. I'd passed it on to my children, Nicole and Toby. Jen was learning it as well and progressing rapidly.

Keeping the doors locked, I signed, "No way." I pointed to the passenger seat.

She gave me a finger sign that isn't technically part of ASL and started around the front of the car. I caught a hint of a smile on her face, which made me nervous. She was planning something—it's hard to keep secrets from a twin.

Carly is spectacular. The phrase "all woman" sometimes pops into my head. She's a six-foot-tall Amazon with luscious golden hair, a doubly dimpled smile, deep blue eyes, and an attention-grabbing figure.

I didn't unlock the door until after she'd tried to open it. She got in.

"Seat belt," I said. "Sorry, Carly, the insurance company made me sign something that said I'd never, ever let you drive."

"Very funny." She took the cup of water I'd placed in the cupholder and started drinking.

I punched the accelerator, timing it just right so the water flew out over her face, splashed onto her elegant white blouse, and made her swallow wrong.

While coughing and spluttering, she signed, "Yeah, go ahead and laugh now, bro. You know I'm going to get you back for that."

"I only wish I had it on video."

She laughed in spite of herself. "I'll send you the dry cleaning bill."

"Oh, right. Yeah, water really stains." I wasn't as good as she was at signing with one hand, but since Nick—the name I'd given the car—was doing the driving, I had both hands free.

We were on our way to a special event at the Fieldbrook Winery. Carly and I are soul mates, but that doesn't mean we always get along. I often need a break from her, given her delusional recklessness, but at that time, we were experiencing a period of détente. It was good for me. I'm fortunate that Jen isn't jealous of the relationship I have with my twin.

"So tell me about this event," I said.

Carly took a pack of grape Trident gum from her purse, unwrapped a piece, and put it in her mouth. She tossed the pack onto the center console. "It's a celebrity wine tasting thing."

"And they invited you by mistake." My twin is a journalist and the author of a best-selling thriller.

She ignored me. "They invited local celebrities and famous oenophiles." She fingerspelled "oenophiles" so fast I only got it by guessing from the context.

"Show-off."

"So, I thought I'd take my baby brother, who only gets to hang out with scummy criminals." Carly is five minutes older than I am.

"Good idea."

She frowned and cocked her head.

"You need me there so I can wrestle you to the ground when you get drunk and boisterous and try to dance on the tables." I took the pack of gum and pulled out a piece.

"I've never done that."

"Oh, really?" I said. "I guess the senior prom is just a hazy memory for you. I wonder why."

"I didn't *try* to dance on the tables. I *did* dance on the tables. Do or do not. There is no try."

"Tomato, tomahto." I just signed "tomato" twice, but Carly got it.

"And I seem to remember you dared me to do it."

"I—*ach*—this gum!" I lowered the window and spit it out. "What the hell is that?" I picked up the pack. "It tastes like …"

She stared at me with a big smile. Full dimples. She fluttered her eyelashes. "Play-Doh?"

"Ah, jeez." I picked up the pack. "You sliced up Play-Doh and wrapped it."

She bared her teeth like a grinning chimp, her wad of gum between her upper and lower incisors.

"Except for the piece you took. Okay, okay, you got me. You have way too much time on your hands. Writer's block?"

"Not at all. Someone has to get you to snap out of it."

"Snap out of what?"

"You're depressed again."

"Do I look depressed?" An implied denial. Lawyer trick. "Who told you that?"

"Nicole. But you seem okay to me. Maybe I'm a good influence on you."

"You are."

"I am?"

"When I'm with you, I feel normal. By contrast."

She waggled her head. "Ha ha. But what do you have to be depressed about, really? You have a beautiful wife who's much younger than you deserve. Wonderful kids who love you and a sister who tolerates you."

"How generous of you."

"I'm serious, bro."

"About tolerating me?"

"I'm serious that you need to stop obsessing over it."

"You brought it up," I said.

"It's kind of childish, really."

I don't know what it is about people in the deaf community—they're often blunt to the point of rudeness.

"Okay, fine." I turned to her. "You're wrong, but you're right, too." Wrong that I could just snap out of it, but right that I gave my moods too much attention.

She fluttered her eyelashes and patted her cheek, congratulating herself.

"So," I said, "message received."

When we got to the winery, Carly picked up the pack of faux gum and put it in her purse.

"What are you going to do with that?"

"I'm going to leave it on a table. Watch what happens." Typical reckless behavior from my crazy sister.

"Seriously? No. Forget it. I know it's harmless, but someone else might see it as poisoning or terrorism. Like putting needles in Halloween candy. Someone's kid might pick it up."

"The evil Play-Doh murderer strikes again." But she tossed it back onto the center console.

Having saved Carly from a lawsuit or criminal prosecution, I got out, went around, and opened her door. She joined me and took my arm.

When we entered the tasting area, I found out what movie stars feel like. Every eye in the place turned to us —well, to Carly. I won't say that all talking stopped, but there was a dip in the noise level.

I wore one of my more stylish gray suits, which, in Humboldt, might as well have been a white tux and tails. Carly wore her silk blouse with a few too many buttons undone, a charcoal pencil skirt, and deadly spike heels. A diamond earring dangled from each ear.

I counted three open jaws, and one of the tasters spit out his wine. Not from shock, admittedly. He spit his mouthful of wine into one of those gross wine spit buckets that all the pros use. I thought there might be some fancy French name for them, but Googling showed me that's what they're called. Wine spit buckets. I'd never used one, but since I was the designated driver, I'd be trying it. I made a mental note to watch some of the snobs to get a feeling for the proper technique.

Many of the imbibers recognized Carly. She'd gotten press coverage in some of the local papers both for her book and as an important person in the deaf community. Bizet University, in Redwood Point, is the top school in the country for deaf students, and as a result, Humboldt has a sizable deaf population.

The grounds of the Fieldbrook Winery were easily the most elegant of any establishment in the area. It was a popular venue for weddings. Trees in different shades of green filtered the sunlight that fell on the lawn, and a redwood burl tasting bar extended across the cement patio and past a gurgling fountain. They had risked bad weather by having the event on May 1 but had lucked out with cool air and warm sunshine.

Carly detached herself and went over to converse with two of her deaf acquaintances. I spied my frenemy, Slater the Waiter.

Derek Slater was the top assistant district attorney in Humboldt County. I can generally count on him to do the right thing, but he sometimes engages in stupefyingly unscrupulous legal behavior that is hard to ignore. He can shift from lovable golden retriever to sneaky Doberman pinscher when you least expect it. His nickname comes from his tendency … to wait … dramatically … between phrases, like William Shatner. His Captain Kirk impression kills at parties. He's in his early fifties, and his bulbous nose and weight problem only seem to endear him to juries—unfortunately for me. Slater's attire was even more formal than mine, but he'd added a flamboyant touch: a fluorescent-green tie that matched the neatly folded handkerchief in his breast pocket, the vertical stripes on his shirt, and his green eyes.

He came over to me, holding two glasses of wine. "So which … do you like better, Goodlove? The pinot or the chardonnay?"

"Remind me, which is the red one?"

"Beats the hell out of me. This one"—he held up the glass in his right hand—"has a musty oak essence, lightly overlaid with a hint of ripe vanilla beans, guava rind, and blueberries grown on the north side of a hill and harvested by naked Russian prostitutes." He held up the other one. "This one tastes like grape Kool-Aid but with less sugar." He tossed it back and smacked his lips.

"I'm partial to the merlot." I pronounced it *mer-lott*.

"Where you been, buddy? I've missed you."

I shrugged. "Taking a well-deserved break."

"Bad news for your scuzzy clients, I guess."

Slater and I bantered for a while until he left. Carly came over to the tasting bar carrying two stools. She set them up, and we became the only two people sitting. Keeping my eyes on her, I swizzled my mouthful of wine around then expertly squirted it into the stainless spit bucket.

Carly laughed, obviously under the influence of the wine she'd been tasting. "I'm going to the bathroom." She toddled off, touching chairs and other things as she passed, aiding the inebriated balance receptors in her inner ear.

I beckoned one of the servers over, a buxom young woman who would have fit in better at Oktoberfest. I whispered in her ear. She gave me a strange look then smiled.

Carly returned, and Ms. Oktober poured us each another glass. The serving sizes were increasing as the end of the event neared. The wind had picked up, and only a few oenophiles remained.

I pointed to the spit bucket. "That's a lot of fancy wine that goes to waste."

My twin sense let me intuit what she'd say next, and she didn't disappoint.

She jabbed her chin toward it. "I dare you to drink some."

"Gross. No way." I poked my index finger toward my mouth and acted as though I were gagging. I waited.

"I'll make it worth your while."

"Not happening. Not even close." I took another mouthful of my wine, gargled with it, and spit it into the bucket.

Carly said nothing, looking out over the garden. Now she was waiting.

I counted to fifteen in my head. Then, "How would you make it worth my while?"

"I'll carry your surfboard for a month."

That was a bigger deal than you might think. Our favorite surf spot requires a long trek down a steep trail, and longboards are heavy. The trip back up can be brutal.

I shook my head. "No. Forget it."

"Two months," she said.

"And you'll clean and rinse my wet suit after every trip?" That was a cold, unpleasant job, especially when worn out from a tiring session. "And hang it up?"

Her eyebrows lifted since she hadn't expected me to accept her dare. She grabbed and shook my hand before I could change my mind. "Deal!"

"Now, wait a second—"

"No, you agreed. We shook on it."

I looked toward the winery's pond, regret written all over my face. I sighed. "Okay." The stainless bucket had a funnel-like top. I removed it, and we both peered over the edge. There was almost a full bottle's worth in there along with who knows how much saliva.

I picked it up with two hands.

Carly slapped me on the shoulder then signed, "No, you'll just pretend to drink it. You have to pour it into a glass and drink the whole glass."

With defeat on my face, I took my empty glass and filled it halfway with wine from the bucket.

Carly snatched the bucket from me and filled the wineglass to the brim.

I held my nose and started to lift the glass then put it down. "Just to be clear, if I drink the contents of this glass, you'll carry my surfboard for two months, and clean, rinse, and hang up my wet suit after every surfing trip we go on together. No other conditions."

"Stop stalling. And if you spit it out or puke, the bet is off."

Holding my nose, I drank half the glass, then put it down and gagged a few times. I stamped my foot. After a deep breath, I drank the rest and swallowed. I held on to the edge of the bar and took deep breaths as if trying to keep it down.

A server at the other end of the bar had his mouth open in horror, but the buxom barmaid just giggled.

Carly looked from her to me. Then to her. Then to me. The penny dropped. "Oh, crap. The bet's off."

"It is not. I followed the conditions of our oral contract faithfully."

"Damn lawyers. What, you had her pour a bottle of wine into a clean bucket, and that's what you drank?"

"Admit it, Sis. I'm the master."

Driving back, I was lost in my thoughts. In the past, I'd thought having a good day meant that a bad one was on the horizon. But I no longer believed that—I wasn't bipolar like my son, Toby. I looked over at Carly, texting with her many friends.

Are relationships the key to beating depression? Perhaps they are a distraction that prevents obsession with—

My phone chimed and the text *Call from Arthur Toll* appeared on the car's screen.

I answered via the hands-free interface. "Garrett Goodlove. Are you okay, Arthur?"

"Hello, Mr.—Garrett. Yes, I am well. I apologize for the tardiness of this request, coming, as it does, on the eve of the day in question, but I wish to revise my answer, or more accurately, reverse it, related to your gracious offer of instruction."

It took me a few seconds to figure out what he was talking about. Or, as he might put it, the matter to which he was referring. "Ah, you would like to come surfing tomorrow, after all."

"Well, based on the preliminary research to which I've devoted no small amount of time, the outing would likely involve, for my part, floundering in the waves rather than surfing per se, but yes, I would like to request, if it is still convenient to your schedule, a lesson in the art of surfing."

"Wonderful, Arthur. Yes, my daughter and I would enjoy having you join us."

"I am most appreciative, Garrett. In addition, I would like to request, and I hope that you will feel no reticence in denying this additional petition, that I bring a friend who shares my desire to learn to surf."

"The more, the merrier. Yes, by all means, bring your friend."

We set up a time and place to meet.

That night, I reviewed the day Carly and I had spent together. I'd felt pretty good. Lying in bed, looking at the ceiling, I had a revelation: On a bad day, I sincerely wished I were dead. On a good day, I didn't wish for that but felt that if I died, for example, in a car crash, I'd be okay with that.

Chapter Three

ARTHUR'S FRIEND TURNED OUT to be an energetic Frenchwoman by the name of Margaux Marchand. She pronounced her Rs in the French way, as if the letters got stuck momentarily in her throat, and the Heimlich maneuver might be required. She pronounced her last name with three syllables. "Mar[choke]shahn-de."

In her late twenties, she had two defining characteristics. The first was her tightly coiled curls, like hundreds of old-fashioned telephone cords plugged into her scalp. They were brown and long enough that I wondered whether it would be hard to wrangle them into the hood of a wet suit. Second, she was big. Well proportioned, but perhaps six foot three. As a child, my best friend and I played with action figures—definitely not dolls—that were from different sets, one being significantly larger. That's what it was like with Margaux. She was from a larger set of action figures.

And the word "action" was appropriate as well. When Nicole and I pulled into the parking lot of Salty's Surf Shop, Margaux was stretching—rotating her upper body side to side, touching her toes, arching her back. We got out, and Arthur introduced us. Margaux's expressive face never seemed to take a break, and it was a pleasure to watch her smile, wink, frown, and laugh as she talked.

"I am so happy to learn the surfing. Thank you very much." The word "happy" sounded like "hoppy" with the accent on the second syllable.

A beginning surfer needs much more strength and endurance than an old hand, since paddling technique and wave savviness give you much more bang for your muscle bucks, but the look of Margaux's upper arms told me she'd have no trouble.

None of the women's wet suits were large enough for the French firecracker, but Salty found a men's large that fit her. It didn't have a hood, but she insisted that it "wouldn't be zee problem."

While Margaux was in the changing room, I asked Arthur if she was his girlfriend.

He blushed, "While one might wish it were so, the nature of our employment, being that I am her supervisor, precludes a personal relationship of a sexual nature, so we are, at this point in time, only work colleagues. Confidentially"—he lowered his voice —"she is an exceptionally strong-willed woman, and I find her difficult to manage."

"Ah, so she is working on the amnesia drug with you."

"Correct, but I would like to request, Garrett, and this is also a directive to all employees from the top management of Vanovax, that you not refer to it as such, but rather simply as 'propolofan.' The CEO, Dr.

Vanhanna, feels, and rightly so, that the term 'amnesia drug' could be interpreted in a pejorative light."

For the newbies, we rented two large soft-topped boards, referred to as "airplane wings" by experienced surfers. Larger boards made it easier to catch and ride a wave, but they were less maneuverable. We put the boards in the bed of Nicole's pickup and drove the few miles to Moonstone Beach. Nicole and I changed into our wet suits—our two students hadn't taken theirs off at the surf shop—and we all hiked across the sand to the water's edge.

It was a gray day, with drizzle drifting in toward us, carrying with it the scents of seaweed and salt water and a hint of dead fish. Seagulls cried overhead, and the wind brought a sound I didn't particularly care for: the barks of sea lions. Sharks loved to dine on blubbery sea lions and seals, and most shark attacks on surfers stem from mistaken identity.

Arthur looked out at the waves. He made the sign of the cross.

"Are you a religious man, Arthur?" I asked.

"While I do not attend services with any degree of regularity, I am steadfast in my commitment to follow the tenets of Christianity and use them to guide my actions."

"It looks scarier than it is." *Wait until he gets out there.*

He looked at the breakers again. "I must admit to a degree of trepidation, but I am eager to begin."

"Eager" was an understatement for Margaux, who seemed ready to rush out into the water without us. "Zees will be the fun clusterfuck, no?"

Nicole laughed, and I racked my brain trying to figure out what word she'd confused the term with. No one ever used that term in a positive sense. Arthur blushed.

My capable daughter placed Arthur's board on the sand, stretched out on it, and began ground school training. "This is how you lie on the board. For now, we'll push you off to catch a wave, but when you graduate from that, you will paddle like this." She demonstrated stroking her hands along the top of the sand. "Paddle, paddle, paddle, and when the board starts to move on its own, you will push down with your hands and pop up to a standing position." She demonstrated. "Try to go from lying down to standing in one movement. If you first rise to your knees, that will be a hard habit to break later on."

She demonstrated a few more times, then it was Margaux's turn. She did surprisingly well and made me wonder whether her upper arm strength was greater than mine. Arthur also did well, although his first pop-up was to his knees.

Nicole and I left our boards on the beach for the time being. We got the scientists' leashes attached to their ankles and headed out into the Pacific.

"Important," I yelled over the sound of the rushing white water. "Don't put the board between you and the wave. It can smash back into you."

Fortunately, someone learning to surf need not go very far out. After a wave has broken, the white water continues to the shore and has plenty of energy to propel a surfer in front of it, especially with the large, floaty boards that beginners use.

When we were waist-deep in the water, Margaux climbed onto her board, which was pointed in toward shore, a huge smile on her face.

"Okay, get ready." Nicole yelled. "Here it comes."

The white water came surging toward us, and Nicole pushed the board along with it. The board's tail rose up, and it started to move, but the nose dug itself into the water. Margaux slid off the front like a pancake off a spatula. She flipped butt over head but jumped up quickly, shaking her telephone cords. "Ooh la la!" Another wave knocked her down.

The next time she was too far back on her board, and the white water passed her by, but the third time everything clicked. The board slid along the front of the foam, and she popped up, standing for three seconds before the board turned, and she fell off with a yell. She got to her feet and jumped up and down, her arms in the air.

We clapped and cheered. Arthur yelled, "Brava!"

While Nicole continued working with Margaux, I went through the same training with Arthur. To my surprise, he got up onto his knees on the very first wave, and on the next one, he popped up and rode all the way in until the fin grounded itself on the sand. He stood and waved, checking that Margaux had seen his performance.

Soon the two neophytes were able to catch the white water on their own, and Nicole and I retrieved our boards and paddled out beyond the breakers. I got there first because even though my muscles are older than hers, my arms are longer, and I'm more experienced with the surfer tricks used to break through the incoming waves. We were both out of breath since getting "outside" at Moonstone was always difficult.

When she reached me, she said, "What a clusterfuck."

I laughed. "What do you think she meant?"

"No idea. Margaux is one wild woman."

"Carly would like her. Can you imagine what kind of trouble they would get into together?" I turned to follow Nicole's gaze and watched a big roller coming toward us.

"You," I said.

I paddled out, and she in, catching it easily, riding for a while, then flipping up into the air when she turned her board seaward.

"Nice!" I yelled.

I caught the third wave after that one. It had a perfect shape, and I was able to execute a few turns then walk up to the nose of the board, briefly hanging five. I continued riding after the wave broke, jumping off when I got to Arthur and Margaux. Both appeared to be having the time of their lives. Margaux had just given Arthur a quick hug, which he didn't return.

"Fun, right?" I yelled.

"*C'est formidable!*" Margaux yelled back.

Arthur gave me two thumbs up.

I struggled my way out again, and Nicole showed off by zipping past me with only a foot or two to spare. The sun came out, and the two of us got in lots of excellent rides. After two hours, my arms were turning into rubber tubing. Tumbling off one wave I'd caught too late, I came to the surface and blinked. Margaux was paddling toward Nicole. *How did she do that?*

Battling out through the surf is a skill that can take years to develop—learning to judge the waves and take advantage of the lulls between sets, for example. With a big, floaty beginner's board, it's usually impossible. Apparently, the big European had just muscled her way through. *Impressive!*

I paddled over to them and pointed to Margaux's head.

She put her fingertips to her forehead then pulled them down and looked at her hand. "Ooh la la!" Blood dripped off her hand and into the water.

"What happened?" I asked.

"I fall, like this—" she jerked her head toward the water "—I guess I hit zee bottom."

That sharks can smell a drop of blood from miles away is a myth, but there could have been a great white right below us for all we knew. As usual, I was less worried about getting killed by a shark than about losing an arm or leg.

I said, "We should probably head in."

"But I get the hang of zees. I pee in zee wet suit. Is okay?"

"Yes. Everyone does that. We can rinse off the suit in the shallows when we're done. Let's head in."

"Is nice and warm."

No amount of argument could get her to come in with us. There was no way I'd leave her out there alone, blood dripping into the water. I got pretty graphic about the shark attacks that had happened right where we were, but it failed to impress her. *Now I see why Arthur says she's hard to manage.*

When the biggest wave of the day rolled ominously toward us like the world's largest steamroller, I thought of a solution. I jumped off my board, my legs tingling as they anticipated the chomp of a car-sized shark. I turned Margaux's board toward shore and yelled, "Get ready."

With the wave feathering, I shoved the board with all my strength. She got a few seconds of an exhilarating ride then tumbled off into the monster washing machine that held her under for almost half a minute. She came to the surface, choking and coughing.

That oughta curb her enthusiasm.

Au contraire.

She waved at me with that big smile of hers before another wave knocked her under. She tried to paddle back out, but the swells were getting larger, and the next three rollers carried her in to where Arthur was practicing. Nicole and I joined them, and our arguments finally broke through her stubbornness. Our reasoning carried more weight when combined with the prospect of fighting her way outside again. She didn't hold it against us and got one more good ride on the white water, staying on the board until it jerked to a stop in the sand, throwing her forward into an inelegant face-plant.

She jumped up, wiped the wet sand off her face, and yelled, "*C'est merveilleux. Merci beaucoup!*"

She continued playing around in the shallow water while Nicole, Arthur, and I walked up the beach to where the sand was dry and flopped down.

"Good session," Nicole said.

We let our black wet suits soak up the warmth of the sun. As happens most days, the wind off the ocean picked up, the cool marine layer rushing to replace warm, rising air inland. Arthur sat cross-legged, and I lay back on the sand.

I put my hands behind my head. "Tell me about your research."

"We're making considerable progress," Arthur said. "My basic hypothesis is that if we can contrive to rid someone of his or her traumatic memories, even if we have to eliminate, at the same time, their normal episodic memories, then, in the case of subjects with severe, untreatable depression, we might have a new therapeutic tool. I must reiterate, however, that mine is still early research on animal models, and I—wait, would you like to come to my lab? I expect that you would find it singularly fascinating."

"I would enjoy that. Thank you, Arthur."

We all peeled off our wet suits in preparation for rinsing them in the shallow water. Arthur's jaw dropped, his face red, and I turned to see what he was looking at. Margaux had worn nothing under her suit. She skipped through the shallow water as if she were the only person on Earth. After dragging the suit through the water, she cavorted around joyously. She had a voluptuous, larger-than-life body that any porn star would envy.

"Ooh la la!" I said.

The next day, Arthur met me at the door to his office and welcomed me with a bow. I'd expected the room to be lined with shelves of scientific books and bound journals, but he explained that everything was digitized, accessible on his computer or tablet. The primary feature of the room was a wall-filling whiteboard packed with molecular formulas. Lots of Cs, Hs, Os, and Ns connected with single or double lines or at the vertices of hexagons. Also, equations such as $C_6H_5CH_3 + 3Cl_2 \rightarrow 3HCl$ and so on. The only thing I recognized was H_2O. I resisted the urge to gesture at the board and ask, *You really understand all this?* The room smelled of dry erase marker.

Arthur hobbled back to his desk, opened a drawer, and pulled out a bottle of pills. He shook three into his palm. "Would you care to join me?"

"Advil?" I smiled. "No, I'm good."

He nodded and swallowed the pills with a sip from his water bottle. "I cannot express to you the severity of the soreness of every muscle in my body, but particularly the latissimus dorsi and obliques." He pointed to his side. "I take it your muscles have habituated to surfing."

"If I haven't surfed for a while, I'll get sore, but remember also that after surfing for years, you develop an economy of style. You don't have to work as hard. It's all in the wrist."

"Yes, I can understand that."

I pointed at the whiteboard. "You're not worried I'll steal company secrets?"

"I … ah … would think—"

I laughed. "You don't have to say it. There's no way I'd understand any of that. I'm joking."

"Would you like the full presentation?"

"I would, but first, I'd like to request, once again, that you consider going to the police with your concerns—" I put up my hands when I saw his frown. "No, no, it's okay. I just had to ask."

"Are you ready for my presentation?"

"I am."

He arched his shoulders with a groan. "Although there is considerable complexity in both the relevant brain anatomy and neuropsychopharmacology, the underlying concept in my research is simple: Can we, someday in the future, create a drug that would make a severely depressed person forget the traumatic event or events which precipitated his illness, and would that cure him or her?"

"Could the drug remove only the traumatic memories?"

"Unlikely. We predict that it will distinguish, to some extent, between semantic memory, like remembering the capital of New Jersey, versus episodic memory, such as remembering a trip to the zoo."

"So, memories of one's life experiences would get thrown out?"

"Quite so," he said. "Although it's possible that an incomplete erasure of the traumatic memories might be enough to blunt their impact on the patient's mood."

"But who would submit to having their memories— their very identity—wiped completely?"

"Someone with major depression. Someone whose life consists entirely of trudging around in a locked ward like a walking vegetable, his or her thoughts tamped down by a daily regimen of powerful psychoactive drugs. Or someone who sits and stares at the floor all day. Have you ever seen someone like that?"

"I have not."

He nodded. "Count yourself lucky. It is an experience which is not easily erased." He shuddered. "But that's the kind of poor soul who may someday benefit from propolofan."

"I'm guessing you don't experiment on people."

"Correct. There are plans to work with monkeys, but that is something I personally wish to avoid. I am perhaps too soft-hearted in that regard. I recognize the monumental eventual benefit to mankind, and the animals are treated humanely, yet I identify with them too much. The research would require subjecting them to a traumatic event. Necessary, but not for me." He shuddered again.

"So what does the research involve?"

He stood. "Let's go to the lab, and I'll show you."

We walked down the hall, and Arthur was greeted by several passing workers in lab coats. One stopped to get his signature on something, and the two talked in biomedicalese for a minute. She was small, with a pixie haircut and a twinkle in her eye. As she was walking away, she winked at me. "Don't let him pull any practical jokes on you."

We continued down the hall, and I turned to Arthur. "You don't seem like a practical joker."

"It was a habit which, with regret, I was forced to cure myself of when I came to appreciate that not everyone likes that form of humor. One's reputation, however, is not easily revised."

I jumped when Margaux snuck up and pinched me on the butt.

"I enjoyed very much the surfing, Garrett. I think maybe I buy a surfboard. I go now." She trotted down the corridor.

Watching her, I couldn't help picturing her naked, voluptuous body capering around in the surf.

Arthur watched also, shaking his head. "She is very intelligent and a hard worker, but managing her is like trying to supervise a tiger while clasping only its tail. In addition, she has an incorrigible propensity toward flirtation."

"She's a very interesting woman."

"That is indisputable." Arthur opened a door and whispered, "We should keep our voices down in this room so as not to disturb the rats."

A number of mini-fridge-sized boxes were distributed around the room, each with a video camera mounted above it. There were no sounds, and the pleasant scent of cedar shavings filled the space.

Arthur pointed to a video screen showing a rat in one of the boxes, a small video screen in front of it. "The experiments are controlled by computer. That rat is called Reggie, and he is being tested on a memory task. Reggie was taught to recognize particular images on the screen in front of him, pressing a lever only when a square appears … okay, now, there's a square and … nothing."

"He failed the test?"

"Yes, he did fail, and that's good." Arthur addressed a young assistant in a light blue lab coat. "How's Reggie doing?"

"Almost zero retention."

"Excellent." Arthur turned back to me. "Reggie was very good at that task before we injected him with propolofan. Since then he has forgotten what he'd learned."

"But pressing levers and seeing square symbols doesn't seem particularly stressful to me."

"Quite so. We are determining the amnesic effects on nontraumatic memory as well as traumatic." He led the way out of the lab. "We create traumatic memories in the rats using—"

"Pictures of hungry cats."

He laughed. "No. It's unpleasant and involves loud noises and electrical shocks. Some rats are—well, I don't wish to recount it since it bothers me, but suffice it to say the rats that undergo this treatment, to express it flippantly, are not happy campers. They exhibit less motor activity, much like the behavior of the person in a locked ward that I described."

"I'm guessing that animal rights activists have a problem with that."

"Quite true. Some of us have been threatened. I understand their feelings, and I must frequently remind myself of the great benefit our experiments may someday yield."

"So does the propolofan cure the depressed rats?"

"I'd remind you that we can't really call them depressed. We can say only that they exhibit symptoms characteristic of human depression. But to answer your question, however, yes, these rats have increased motor activity and exhibit more social interaction with other rats as compared to those in the control group, who received only a saline injection. In addition, we've shown a clear dose-response curve, meaning, in lay terms, that the drug is more effective at a higher dose, up to a point."

"So, it's working."

Arthur nodded. "In our animal models, yes, it's working."

I watched the rat happily working away. *Could a drug like that work for me?*

Chapter Four

LOUELLA SAT IN HER home office and typed a search string into her browser. She was a hunt-and-peck typist, but fast. She thought back to being a detective in the days before the internet and shook her head. *The dark ages.*

The room was dim and cramped, just the way she liked it. She and her husband had purchased the Victorian in 2003 when she'd joined the RPPD. It could have starred in an episode of *This Really Old House*.

She took a break to appreciate the decor. When they'd moved in, she'd given her granddaughter, fourteen at the time and aspiring to be an interior designer, free rein in setting up the office. Jasmine had painted the walls a sage green and filled them chockablock with a mismatched variety of objects. For example, a small mirror, a photo montage of her family, a shot of Louella's graduation from the LAPD police academy in 1974, and a photograph showing the day in 1979 when she'd made detective. Two signs concerned her smoking —Jasmine was trying to get her nana to quit. The first showed Uncle Sam pointing and the caption *I want you to put out that cigarette.* The second showed a cigarette overlaid with a red circle with a diagonal red line. It read, *Cancer Cures Smoking.*

Louella puffed out a cloud of vapor that was bigger than a breadbox. *At least Jasmine never took up the disgusting habit.* Louella's husband had quit, but it was too late for him. He died of lung cancer only one year after his retirement.

Chimes from the mantel clock downstairs pulled her from her reverie, and she clicked on the top search result, *Vanovax Soon to Bring Cheaper Vaccine to Market.* She read the article. The current vaccines against COVID-19 were expensive, the most popular coming in at over $400 for a set of three shots and requiring revaccination every few months. Vanovax's replacement would require only a single dose and cost no more than a flu shot. Although its effectiveness might be as low as seventy percent, it was likely to be a cash cow for the company.

But a payday in the billions was a recipe for corruption. Garrett had suggested that some hanky-panky was going on in the company, something serious enough to put a whistleblower in danger. She squinted. *But how would fraud work in that situation?* He admitted that she might be chasing a wild biomedical goose, but Louella used one of her investigative tricks: She imagined she already knew there was something to find, but she just didn't know what it was.

After three more hours of internet research, Louella put on her harried reporter personality and dialed the company, whose campus was ten miles south of

Redwood Point. The telephone system dumped her back to a dial tone three times. *This is why I make the big bucks.* Finally, she got through to the public relations officer, a Mr. Vincent Spassowsky, whose Facebook page was open in front of her. His cover photo was a selfie taken at what appeared to be a spring break wet t-shirt contest. His huge mirrored sunglasses showed his arm stretched out and holding his phone. He had peach fuzz on his chin and pimples on one cheek.

"This is Mr. Spassowsky."

Louella suppressed the desire to ask why the hell he hadn't changed his name. "Mr. Spassowsky, this is Loretta Marcus from the *Shreveport Times*." She emphasized her Southern accent. "We're planning a cover story on Vanovax. I've been impressed with the amount of publicity your company has received lately. Is that your doing?"

"I work very hard, Ms. Marcus."

"We're most interested in this new vaccine you're bringing to market. The VVD9 vaccine. Our readers would like to know how you'll be able to produce it at such a reasonable price."

"I'm very glad you asked that, Ms. Marcus. We've been able to harness the latest in innovative vaccine platform technologies, which gives us a way to target a new pathogen rapidly, like changing a cartridge in a video game console."

Louella wasn't sure if the kid really knew his stuff or had just memorized some techie phrases. It didn't matter. Her goal was to butter him up enough that he'd grant her an interview with the head of the company.

"Excellent," she said. "Give me just a second to write that down."

Louella's seven-week-old kitten clawed its way up her leg and began meowing. More like little squeaks. Louella could almost hear Spassowsky frown.

"You say you're with the *Shreveport Times*?" he asked.

"We have a significant online presence." She laughed. "One of the reporters just brought her kitten into the office, and it's cute as a cupcake." Louella petted Lisbeth, who settled into her lap and began purring.

After more questions and some serious ass-kissing, Louella achieved her goal: an interview with Rita Vanhanna, the founder and CEO of Vanovax.

She took off her headset and held the kitten against her cheek. "I hate to lie, Lisbeth, but it's part of the job."

I sat at our conference table, a piece of furniture that was over a hundred years old and looked it. I'd tried restoring it myself but gave up and turned the job over to a pro. She'd recommended putting a new top on, but that, I felt, defeated the purpose of having a genuine antique in the room. She did a good job of making a silk purse out of the heavy-as-a-hog conference table, but it was more of a conversation piece than something that would elicit oohs and ahs on *Antiques Roadshow*.

I listened to how the clicks coming from the radiator matched the ticking of the grandfather clock in the corner.

"Dad!"

"Sorry, sweetheart." I sat up. "Go ahead."

Nicole and Jen exchanged glances.

Nicole said, "I wanted to know if there's something about Arthur's situation that we are unaware of."

I frowned. "No … I've told you everything. What do you mean?"

"Well, I don't … I can't see anything that would warrant having Louella investigating Vanovax. At this point, Arthur has simply given us a letter to hold for him. He didn't ask us to take any action other than to put it in a safe place, so I'm wondering if you know something we don't."

I rubbed my hand down my face. "We can certainly afford it."

"You put me in charge of operations and cash flow, and I can't see *we can afford it* as a valid reason for a significant and unnecessary expenditure."

I glanced at Jen, who was looking down at her legal pad—probably not wanting to make it seem that she and Nicole were ganging up on the company slacker.

I took a breath, noticing Jen's perfume. "Okay, here's my reasoning. You don't give a letter like that to a lawyer unless you perceive a threat. *In the event that something happens to me.* That implies a serious threat. You wouldn't do that if you thought someone might simply beat you up. You'd only do it if you thought you might be killed. Right?"

They both nodded, Nicole a little more reluctantly than Jen.

"Arthur doesn't want me to go to the police. That is stupid, and one of the roles I see of an attorney is to protect the client from doing stupid things." I held up my hands. "I know you're thinking that this is just my overactive curiosity, and I admit that's part of it. But think of it this way. Remember when we gave Louella the kitten?"

"That she said she didn't want, but now loves," Jen said.

"Right. So what did that kitten do when we put her on the floor? She started looking around, poking her nose into every nook and cranny. That's curiosity, and by learning about her environment, she's more prepared to respond in an emergency. She knows which cranny to run to if an enemy appears."

Nicole clicked her pen. "Curiosity saves the client."

"Something like that, yeah. So by researching now, we'll be a jump ahead if something does happen to him."

"But you had Louella investigate Vanovax. The threat could be from something else entirely. A neighbor, for example."

"True," I said, "but I got the impression Arthur doesn't have much of a life outside of his work. I could be wrong. However, Vanovax seemed like a good place to begin. Louella agreed."

Nicole made a note. "How about we put a cap on that expenditure? Or a time limit."

"Fair enough."

We came up with a figure we all agreed on.

"*Koibito*," Jen said, "there's something else."

"I'm slacking."

She said nothing.

"I never thought that I did this for the money," I said, "but now that we're flush, I'm not as motivated. We've had this conversation before. I can get my act together."

"You can retire if you want, you know. Nicole and I
—"

"No, I don't want that. Just give me a little time. I can beat this."

Miss Smaridge tapped on the door, opened it, and hit the conference table with a disapproving look. "Detective Sergeant Granville is here."

"Edith Granville?" I asked. *What possible reason could she have for a visit?*

Smaridge ignored my admittedly dumb question and left, to be replaced with the imperial figure of Humboldt County's top cop.

I have this thing in my brain: I tend to notice resemblances that others don't. Jen probably gets tired of the type of conversation we'd had a week earlier. I'd said, "Doesn't our waitress look like that woman from *The Office*?"

"Who, Jenna Fischer?" Jen never forgets a name.

"Yeah."

She'd waggled her hand. "I guess so. A little bit."

But in this case, Jen agreed—after I mentioned it— that Edith Granville looked and acted like the dowager countess in *Downton Abbey*, as portrayed by Maggie Smith. Edith had been some kind of inspector with Scotland Yard until she traded the dreary climate of England for the equally dreary climate of Redwood Point. A tall woman in her seventies, she was hale and hearty except for a dodgy leg that forced her to use a cane. Her disapproving looks rivaled those of our legal secretary but were delivered half in jest as part of her subtle deadpan humor. At least I hoped that was the case. Because of her history she was universally referred to as "Inspector Granville."

She stood by the end of the conference table, both hands on the top of her gold-topped cane. "I'm sorry to interrupt, Garrett." Her accent matched her appearance. "I can see you are busy with your endeavors to keep petty criminals in circulation, but a matter has arisen about which you may have some information."

"Would you like a cup of coffee?" I asked.

"Thank you, no. This concerns one of your surfing playmates. An intern at the Vanovax Corporation has filed a missing persons report—"

"Arthur Toll!" I said.

Granville blinked a few times. "Quite so. Do you know where he is?"

I stood and headed for the door. "I'll be right back."

Hurrying up the stairs to my office safe, I heard some of what Inspector Granville said to Jen. It included the words "older husband" and "weak bladder."

Chapter Five

I RETURNED, BRANDISHING ARTHUR'S letter, and found Inspector Granville seated and sipping coffee, her cane on the conference table.

I sat. "Did Jen fill you in?"

"Nicole did. I assume you attempted to convince Dr. Toll to take the matter to the police?"

"I did. He refused. Can you bring me up to date?"

"This morning, a Ms. Kirsten Peak called our department to report a missing person. She said that Dr. Toll is punctual in the extreme and would never fail to show up without calling in. An officer visited the company to take a report. He found Ms. Peak to be prone to exaggeration and conspiracy theories, but he confirmed that Toll's absence was highly unusual. They checked his residence, and he wasn't there. When asked about Dr. Toll's friends, Ms. Peak said he had few or none but had been excited about going surfing with you."

"Anything about a Ms. Margaux Marchand?"

Granville took a small notebook from her pocket and wrote in it. "No. Is she Dr. Toll's lady friend?"

I shook my head. "I don't know. I don't think so. She came surfing with us. Can you tell me why you came here?"

"You mean, why I myself came instead of sending a deputy or phoning?"

"Yes."

"I was across the street meeting with the chancellor of Bizet University on an unrelated matter."

I took the letter opener from a side table, slipped it under the envelope's flap, and cut it open. I slid a few sheets of paper and a check onto the tabletop. The check, drawn from a Vanguard money market fund, was for $50,000 made out to Goodlove and Shek. I pushed that over to Nicole. The top sheet was a letter. I scanned through it.

"Let's see." I cleared my throat. "The letter reads as follows: 'Redwood Point, California, April twenty-eight, 2021. My dear Mr. Goodlove. If you are reading this, I may have been killed or injured in such a way as to render me incommunicado. If such is the case, please allow my suspicions, described herein, to guide an investigation into the vaccine department at Vanovax Corporation. I was hesitant to reveal those suspicions because I considered them insubstantial.'"

I made sure to avoid an I-told-you-so tone. "'On fifteen April, when retrieving stationery from a walk-in supply cabinet, I overheard a conversation conducted sotto voce. The words I could discern were, verbatim, 'The FDA inspectors have their heads up their asses. This is too sophisticated for them. They won't have a clue.' I deemed it wise to conceal my identity and lay doggo in the closet until the corridor was clear."

I turned to Jen. "'Lie doggo' means to hide?"

It was Granville who answered. "Quite so. Very old-fashioned. Did Dr. Toll speak in that antiquated manner?"

"He did." I kept reading. "'My curiosity piqued, I unwisely chose to make inquiries about the FDA testing of our products, attempting to camouflage them as offhand remarks. When doing so in the company cafeteria, two researchers at the neighboring table simultaneously stiffened and turned their heads toward me in a rapid manner. I don't know their names, but I believe they are part of the VVD9 vaccine team. They looked directly at me, and I'm afraid my manner, lacking as I am in the wiles of subterfuge, may have advertised my true purpose.

"'Because my suspicions are based upon these singularly insubstantial data, I have resolved to investigate. If anything happens to me, please provide this letter to the police and use the enclosed check to finance your own investigation. Sincerely, Arthur Toll, April 28, in the year of our Lord 2021, Redwood Point, California. PS: I believe Ms. Margaux Marchand may also suspect misdeeds in the vaccine department.'"

"What are the other sheets?" Jen asked.

I picked them up, checking both the first and second sheets. "Power of attorney form. Looks like something he downloaded from the internet. Let's see … 'Limited Power of Attorney. Be it acknowledged that I, Arthur Toll with a mailing address of' blah blah blah, 'the Principal, do hereby grant a limited and specific power of attorney to Garrett Goodlove of 202 M Street, et cetera as my Attorney-in-Fact. Said Attorney-in-Fact shall have full power and authority to undertake and perform only the following acts on my behalf: Access my property, safe deposit box, bank accounts, act on my behalf in all matters. The authority herein shall include such incidental acts as are reasonably required to carry out and perform the specific authorities granted herein.'"

I looked up. "It seems to be in order, although the 'in all matters' is overly broad."

"Notarized?" Nicole asked.

I flipped to the second page. "Yes."

Granville pointed to the check. "By how much did he overpay you?"

"I'm sorry, you know that's confidential."

"Well, I trust that you will apply much of it to Louella Davis. We shall give her our cooperation."

It's a myth, created by TV screenwriters looking to add conflict to their scripts, that the police are always at odds with private detectives. They frequently work hand in hand. Louella and Granville are friends, respect one another, and frequently share their findings.

"She's already on the case," I said.

Granville frowned. "But how can that be, Garrett? You didn't know he was missing until now."

"An attorney's greatest asset is the ability to foresee the future."

"Oh, rubbish." Inspector Granville stood with the assistance of her cane. On her way out, she turned and said, "I do hope you will endeavor to be less full of yourself, Garrett."

* * *

Dressed in a dark blue business suit with a black pearl necklace, Louella walked into the lobby of Vanovax Corporation. She'd considered scrapping the pretense of being a news reporter. There was now a legitimate reason to investigate the company, so she could have been honest: *I'm an investigator looking into the disappearance of one of your employees.* But the point of the interview was to get a feeling for Rita Vanhanna, the company's founder and CEO, and a more informal interview might work best for that. The goal was the answer to two questions: Was Rita Vanhanna behind this alleged plan to defraud the FDA, and could she be responsible for Arthur's disappearance?

At thirty, Vanhanna was one of the youngest female CEOs of a major corporation in the country. According to media articles, she had one all-consuming passion in her life: virology. She credited that passion for her success, and, in turn, credited her Asperger's for her ability to focus on her chosen subject. She was vocal about her disorder and had done a TED Talk on it two years earlier. Louella decided to use that as an icebreaker.

Five minutes after Louella checked in with the receptionist, Dr. Vanhanna herself came to the lobby. She was more handsome than pretty, slender with a long face and shoulder-length brown hair that might have been combed earlier but was no longer under control. She wore a green pantsuit similar to Louella's outfit.

Louella stood, and the two women greeted one another with bows.

"Please come with me," Vanhanna said without a smile and turned back the way she'd come.

Her office was a restful space with floor-to-ceiling windows and many framed representations of DNA, some artistic, some realistic. The CEO sat behind her desk, and Louella chose a visitor chair.

"I'd like to ask you about what it's like, as someone with Asperger's, to head a company," Louella said.

Vanhanna nodded. "That's fine. In my case, I think of my ASD, which stands for Autism Spectrum Disorder, as primarily a developmental problem."

Louella had expected problems with eye contact or awkwardness, but there were none. The woman spoke quickly.

"The way I think of ASD," she said, "is this: Most people, as they grow up, assimilate the norms of social behavior naturally, through osmosis, if you will. That was not the case for me or for many with ASD. It was as though I'd been dropped into a complex video game but without a manual. I still am unclear on how neurotypicals pick up on those norms. My brain is wired differently, and fortunately, my parents picked up on it very early. They remember the day they read through a list of Asperger's symptoms, saying, 'Yes!' to each. They took me to a psychologist right away. That early diagnosis gave me a tremendous advantage."

There was no need to prompt Vanhanna; her speech flowed as if it had all been written out in advance.

"Because I was diagnosed with ASD at age five, I went through less of a hell than most with the disorder. Without guidance from my therapists, I would have been lost and ostracized even more than was the case. I was simply thought of as 'that weird girl,' but I wasn't totally isolated."

She rocked back and forth slightly as she spoke. "One thing the therapists gave me was a set of scripts on how to behave in different situations. Again, those scripts are not needed for those without ASD. A neurotypical would intuit that an expression such as 'Get outta here!' doesn't mean that one should literally leave the room. Things like that were confusing for me as a child. It was as though I needed to be programmed. I even had charts of different facial expressions with a subroutine to invoke for each. I memorized those scripts.

"As another example, I had to learn how the normal flow of conversation works, and I had to learn to not monopolize the conversation, which I am doing now and apologize for."

"That's quite all right," Louella said. "Could you tell me how much of the day-to-day operation of the company you're involved in?"

"As little as possible. Unlike Bill Gates, who I suspect is also an Aspie, my focus is on one thing. Virology. He, I've heard him say, was obsessed with software but also with hiring people. I have never been involved in personnel, other than choosing a few men and women with extraordinary skill in organization. They, in turn, have hired the best scientific minds in this field."

"What about the division dealing with propolofan?"

"I'm sure you've heard of the disappearance of the lead researcher in that department. That disturbs me greatly. He is well-liked by his colleagues, and his disappearance makes me realize that I should make more of an effort to personally appreciate my employees. He is a phenomenal scientist, and I am keeping my fingers crossed that he will return soon and will be okay. I have reached out to the police to tell them that I would like to help them in any way I can, and I'm putting up a one-hundred-thousand-dollar reward for information leading to his return."

Louella jotted the information down in her notebook. "Back to the virus department. Can you tell me about this VVD9 vaccine you're working on?"

"Yes, that effort is headed up by Dr. Spiker, and the vaccine will soon be approved. We are ready to ramp up production, and Dr. Spiker has been able to design the product in such a way that it will be significantly cheaper to produce than competing products. I really don't know how he does that, and I would look into it if I weren't working on my own project."

"What is that?"

"I'm trying for a cheaper version of the HPV, which is currently the most expensive routine vaccine in the country. I would like to produce one that can be administered in a single dose. It's terribly underutilized now, and I'm hoping that my version will expand its use throughout the world, especially in underdeveloped countries."

"Concerning the VVD9 vaccine. You are not involved at all with that project?"

Vanhanna frowned and cocked her head. "I thought I already mentioned that. No, I am not. Dr. Spiker is extremely capable."

Louella continued the interview, coming to like the genius doctor. *This woman is no criminal.* After they finished up, Louella said she could find her own way out.

In the hall, a quick movement caught Louella's attention. A short woman hurried away and cast a furtive glance toward Louella. The woman gave off a nervous vibe, as if she had been caught doing something wrong. She turned a corner. Louella followed her, but when she got to the corner, the woman was gone.

Louella was halfway home when she noticed, a block behind her, the bright-yellow Toyota Corolla that she'd seen in the Vanovax parking lot. She checked her rearview mirror often. The Corolla kept its distance. *This is interesting.*

Sometimes an investigation is going nowhere, petering out, when the bad guy gets nervous and tips his hand by trying to interfere. Louella made a random turn and watched the mirror. *Yes, there's the yellow car again.* Certainly not a pro. If you're going to follow someone, using a car painted bright, nonstandard yellow is not a good idea.

She changed course again, confirming that she was indeed being inexpertly followed. She parked in Old Town, and it wasn't long before the yellow car came into sight and parked a block away. Unobtrusively, Louella retrieved her gun and holster from the trunk. She slipped the holster on under her suit jacket and seated the weapon. Then she walked along the street and turned into the alley next to Old Town Coffee and Chocolate.

She waited, and soon her pursuer made the turn into the alley. *Definitely not a pro.* She grabbed the collar of the small woman—the same one she'd seen scuttling away in the hall at Vanovax. The girl yelped.

Louella said nothing.

The girl put her hands up and spoke in a quavering voice. "Sorry, I have to talk with you. I was following you because I didn't want anyone to see us together. I was going to talk to you when you got where you were going." She looked around as if the street might be full of spies.

Louella watched her for a few seconds. "Okay, but be good. I have a gun." Mentioning the gun was probably overkill—the girl seemed harmless. "Let's go over here." They went farther into the alley and sat down on some milk crates between the dumpsters. Cigarette butts littered the area, and the place smelled like sour milk and coffee.

"You're a reporter, but you carry a gun?" the girl asked, her voice high and strained.

Louella took out her vape pen, clicked it five times to turn it on, and took a puff. "What's your name?"

"I'm Kirsten Peak, but don't tell anyone that I've talked with you, okay?" The young woman had a pleasant round face with large eyes and more makeup than she needed.

"What is it you want to tell me?"

"I think I know why Dr. Toll disappeared. There's something going on at Vanovax, and I think he was about to figure it out. That's why someone killed him."

"Someone killed him? Do you know that?"

"No," she said. "But I think it's likely. Don't you?"

"Kirsten, you stay right here. Don't get up. I'm going to get my car. I'll drive it into the alley, and you get in, and we'll drive to my house. Will you stay right here?"

"Yes. Yes, I will."

"I know where your car is, so I'll get you if you try to run."

"No, I'll stay here. I promise."

Louella fast-walked to her car and drove into the alley. She doubted the need for the cloak-and-dagger stuff, but there was little downside to being careful. Kirsten got into the passenger seat, reclined it, and lay back. Louella drove around, and after confirming they weren't being followed, proceeded to her home and pulled into the garage.

In the kitchen, Louella poured two whiskeys and sat at the old Formica table. "What have you got?"

"The VVD9 vaccine group is running a scam. It's really big. It's a bit technical."

"I'll try to understand." Louella blew vapor out toward the ceiling. "But first, why did you come to me?"

"You're a reporter, right? An investigative reporter?"

Louella waited.

"I thought I'd be safer if I talked to you instead of going to the police."

"Okay," Louella said. "So, what's this scheme?"

"Right, you remember the Volkswagen scam?"

"Dieselgate?"

"Yeah. You know how that worked?"

Louella sipped her drink, the vape pen between her index and middle fingers. "They rigged the software so that it could detect whenever the government was testing a car's emissions system in a lab and then adjust things so it would pass."

"Right. Exactly. That let them produce cars that passed the emissions tests, but in real-world driving, they polluted a lot. Much more than the testing suggested."

Louella's kitten climbed up onto her lap, and she petted it.

"Well," Kirsten said, "they're doing the same kind of thing with the VVD9 vaccine."

"How? There's no software involved."

"Yeah, it's really genius, and I don't understand it completely. I'm just an intern. The FDA does spot checks on vaccines after they're produced. The group has engineered things so that the individual vials of the vaccine will pass, but they'll be totally useless."

"Why go to that trouble?"

Kirsten frowned. "What do you mean?"

"Why not just produce the real thing? Oh, the fake vaccine is—"

"Cheaper. Much cheaper to produce."

"But that would have to be a huge conspiracy. Everyone would be in on it."

"Not really. Just a few people. It worked for Volkswagen, remember."

"But won't it be immediately apparent that the vaccine isn't doing anything? That people aren't protected?"

"Well, that's the beauty of it. Like the seasonal flu vaccines, the effectiveness of the real vaccine can be as low as fifty percent anyway. So, yeah, maybe they'll figure it out at some point, but it's not like a counterfeit antibiotic or something."

"And by the time they figure it out, tens of thousands might die."

Kirsten nodded. "It's sick is what it is."

Two days after Arthur's disappearance was discovered, I convened a strategy session.

One of the nice things about having a legal secretary born in the 1930s is that she doesn't feel she's above making coffee. Miss Smaridge saw it as an important part of her job description. She disapproved of our single-use Keurig machine, too wasteful—so I ordered a conventional model she liked. Happy legal secretary, happy office.

With the scent of Peet's French Roast in the air, Jen, Nicole, Louella, and I sat around the conference table.

I put my coffee down. "Okay, to summarize, Arthur's disappeared, and Louella has uncovered a strong motive for wanting him gone."

"Is Margaux gone too?" Nicole asked. "They worked together and were friends, right? If someone is worried enough to kill Arthur—"

"Hold on." I put my hand up. "I think it's too early to assume someone killed him."

Nicole leaned back. "I'm not assuming that. Right now, we're looking at the possible consequences of Louella's discovery that someone has a strong motive for keeping Arthur from spilling the beans, and based on that, murder is a clear possibility. What other scenario is there? Kidnapping?"

"I can think of a few," I said.

"Such as?"

"Maybe Arthur is afraid for his life, and he decided disappearing was his safest option."

Jen said, "And he didn't tell his lawyer and new surfing buddy?"

"He only knew me a few days. If it were me and I was really scared, I think I'd just disappear without telling a soul. Plus, he'd given me the letter, so he'd already told us what to do if anything happened. Maybe he'd even planned to disappear."

Louella took the vape pen from her mouth. "He emptied his local checking account on Monday the tenth. Took it out in cash."

"Could someone have forced him to do that?" Nicole adjusted her mug on its coaster.

Louella pursed her lips. "Possible but unlikely. What are you thinking?"

"Blackmail?"

"Let's back up," Jen said. "Louella, I assume you checked whether Margaux is also missing."

Louella said, "She's gone, but she had a planned vacation. None of her colleagues knows where she was going. I'm looking into it."

"That's odd, isn't it?" Jen raised her eyebrows. "She didn't talk about her vacation plans?"

"I get the feeling she's a little unusual."

I thought back to Margaux's naked public cavorting. "In what way, Louella?"

"Just a feeling based on my interviews with the people she worked with. One man thought she was flirting with him, for example."

"That's not so unusual."

"But he was in his sixties," she said.

I laughed. "Maybe she was joking."

"He didn't get that impression. Plus, she's strangely secretive about her private life."

"Okay, so back to Arthur," I said. "I suggest we try to find him."

Jen squinted one eye. "But you think maybe he doesn't want to be found."

"True, but that was just one possibility, and I've reconsidered it. He trusted me, but even if he didn't, he might have at least sent me a text saying he was going to disappear."

"As the devil's advocate," Jen said, "should we leave this up to the police? We're a law firm, not a detective agency. We pay taxes so the police can handle things like this. We read the letter, and you've alerted the police to what you found, right, Louella?"

"Yes, and I've set up a meeting with an FBI contact. He's going to bring in the FDA."

Jen crossed her arms. "So, boss, this is more a police matter than—"

"No," I said, a little more emphatically than I meant to. "Arthur's our client. He's given us fifty thousand to finance an investigation. Plus, he's my friend."

"Of two days."

"Still."

"I have an idea," Nicole said. "I know of an excellent public relations firm. I'll bet they could come up with a press release that would get national coverage. That might turn up something."

I rubbed the back of my neck. "A missing person isn't exactly stop-the-presses news."

Nicole held out her hands as though framing a headline and announced, "Famous Amnesia Doctor Forgets to Go Home."

I laughed. "Do it."

Chapter Six

SPECIAL AGENT RANDOLPH TICK of the FBI and Dr. Edoardo Mazza of the FDA stood when Louella's escort led her into the sterile conference room. She'd worked with Tick briefly, and the man matched the stereotype of an FBI agent. He stood tall, with a flattop haircut, a square jaw, and a conservative suit. Mazza looked more like your typical man on the street, early sixties, poor posture.

The conference room was on the eighteenth floor of the federal building on Golden Gate Avenue, and Louella took a moment to appreciate the dramatic view of San Francisco below. *No views like this in Redwood Point.*

Agent Tick sat. "Shall we get right to it?"

When Louella and Mazza agreed, he continued, "After we talked on the phone, I looked over your report, Ms. Davis. Dr. Mazza has been discussing this with his colleagues, and they've come up with a few ways that their vaccine checks could be fooled. Isn't that right, Dr. Mazza?"

"Yes. Now that we've been presented with the idea that this trickery may exist, my colleagues and I have come up with how it might be done. It's made us realize the deficiencies in our tests, like—" he smacked his forehead "—why didn't we think of that before?"

Louella almost smiled. The man, as educated as he must have been, had a heavy Italian accent.

"You probably weren't expecting deception," she said.

"That's right," he said. *Thatsa righta.* "We see it as working together with the production companies to make sure the vaccines match the highest standards. Not as an adversarial relationship."

"So you think this is a real scam."

"Definitely possible."

"I realize," Tick said, "that your main interest is in your missing person, Dr. Arthur Toll, but—"

"You don't get involved with missing persons unless it's a child or involves interstate travel," Louella said.

"Yes."

"But finding Dr. Toll or locating his body could help with your case against Vanovax."

"True, and we may well pursue it, giving the local authorities help as they request it, but realize we're dealing with a very different timeline. Vanovax is still months away from vaccine production—"

Mazza said, "They still have to go through a lengthy testing process, even if they're going to fudge the results."

"Yes." Tick nodded. "So we have time to do what the government does best, carefully build an airtight case. There's essentially no rush because there will be no harm until Vanovax starts producing the vaccine. At that point, we'll be able to swoop in and catch them red-handed." He paged through his notes. "You don't think Rita Vanhanna is involved?"

"That's my impression, unless she's a very good actor. I would look at this Henry Spiker fellow. He's the lead on the vaccine, and Vanhanna leaves things up to him."

"He certainly *looks* guilty." Tick showed a photograph to Mazza. Spiker was a Goth type, with spiky, greasy black hair and, in the photo, heavy black eyeliner above and below his eyes. He looked nothing like a scientist. Tick turned to Louella. "This guy is some kind of genius?"

"That's what they say."

The three continued their discussion of the case, and Tick promised to share any information that might bear on Arthur's disappearance.

Louella looked out the window. *I'll believe that when I see it.*

But it got worse.

"One more thing," Tick said. "While we conduct our investigation, it's imperative that no one at Vanovax knows about it. We don't want them covering their tracks."

"You realize that puts me in danger."

Tick said nothing.

"Right now, they may assume I'm the only one looking into their fraud. They might have already killed someone to keep their secret. They could decide to knock me off, too."

Tick put a sheet of paper on the table and slid it over to Louella.

She didn't look at it or pick it up. "What's this?"

"Confidentiality agreement."

"And I should sign it because ...?"

"If you sign it, we may be able to spare an agent to protect you. And we'd be more likely to share our findings."

Louella laughed and said her goodbyes.

The weather was perfect for kayak fishing, but I didn't appreciate it. Because there was no wind, my boat slid through the water as if I were traveling downhill. The sun had risen but was still hidden behind the hill of redwoods that came to the edge of the water. I hugged the shore because it showed me how fast I was moving. The booms from the waves breaking on the sandspit between Big Lagoon and the ocean were almost continuous. A saltwater tang drifted in over the spit. We'd had a recent cold snap, and I'd have been freezing without the long underwear I wore beneath my dry suit. I twisted back and looked up as a noisy flock of Canada geese flew over, heading north but saw only fog.

I should have appreciated all of that, but I didn't because I wasn't catching any damn fish. It was my fourth outing without even a nibble. I don't know what's worse: imagining there were no fish down there or picturing them swimming around, ignoring my bait. I've tried to enjoy kayaking for its own sake but gave up on that years earlier.

I stopped paddling when I came to a cove that had been productive in the past. I threaded a fat worm onto the hook—*Sorry, fella*—cast out, and kept my eye on the thin bobber.

I hadn't invited Zach, Carly's boyfriend, because I wanted to spend my time thinking. Nothing like staring at a little piece of Styrofoam, waiting for it to jerk under the water, to give you time for reflection.

Arthur's case was perfect for stealing attention from my state of mind. *The key to happiness.* I decided to drop everything else and concentrate on finding him or finding out what had happened to him. I wouldn't let anything interfere with my … quest. I also wanted to do it for him.

After another hour of unproductive fishing—lures, bait, jigs, nothing worked—I thought about the news article that had come out and immediately gained national attention, as Nicole had predicted it would. The headline read, *Does the World's Top Amnesia Scientist Have Amnesia?* followed by *Some people are speculating that MIT-educated scientist Arthur Toll, who's been developing the world's first amnesia drug, may have gotten a dose of his own medicine.* Typical media sensationalism, although it did have a pleasing symmetry. The best part, for our purposes, was the clear color photo of Arthur, looking like a geeky mad scientist with mild anorexia. The article requested that people contact the Redwood Point Police Department if they had information. It also mentioned the $100,000 reward Vanovax had offered. That should do the trick. *My daughter is a genius.*

I didn't feel like a genius. I was being outsmarted by animals with pea-sized brains, literally. When the wind picked up, I paddled in, empty-handed.

That night, exhausted from a day on the water, I was getting ready to hit the sack when a text came in. I read it. *Oh, crap, not again!*

It was from Toby. *Dad, I figured out I have a superpower. You do too!*

I texted back, *Where are you?*

I waited. No reply. Last I knew, he'd been on a photo shoot in Wyoming.

Comparing Toby's mental illness to mine was like comparing Godzilla to a peeved gecko. Luckily, his monster could be tamed and controlled with medication —as long as he took it. He'd been hospitalized on several occasions, most of which involved a failure to keep up with his pills. His medications, carefully balanced over years of supervised experimentation, allowed him to exist on the edges of both sanity and society. I couldn't imagine him in a nine-to-five job, but his talent at photography gave him a sustainable career.

Many bipolar sufferers fail to take their medication regularly. Some refuse to accept their illness. Others can't handle the side effects or miss the powerful high that the mania gives them. With Toby, I think he veers slightly into manic territory and then, feeling invincible, decides he doesn't need to take his pills. I'm not sure about that—I'm not a doctor. When he goes through one of his episodes, it's hard to get him to explain exactly what happened.

With a text like that, was there a chance he was fine? No. Discovering superpowers is not something that happens to a well person. *Maybe he was joking?*

With no reply after thirty minutes, I texted, *Toby, please go to an emergency room. Carly and/or I will come and meet you there.* I also sent texts to my sister and daughter, alerting them. They would check their schedules to see if they could clear some time to go to wherever Toby was in trouble. They knew the drill.

Still no reply. I'd been on this train before, and the next stop would be a call from the police or a hospital. No telling how far away that station was. I crawled into bed, prepared for a sleepless night. Jen mumbled something and snuggled against me.

Chapter Seven

THE EXPECTED CALL CAME the next morning at 9:30.

"Is this Toby Goodlove's father?"

"Yes! Is he okay?"

"He had a rough night out on a trail, but physically he's fine and will recover. I'm Dr. Jackie Gray, a psychiatrist here at Poudre Valley Hospital—"

"Where is that?" I wrote her name down.

"Ah, sorry. Fort Collins, Colorado. Toby is in the midst of a manic episode, and I take it you're aware of those?"

"Yes." I wrote, *ASAP flight to Fort Collins. Carly and me* on my pad and buzzed the intercom.

"We weren't able to get his name from him until recently, and now we have his records. I'm next going to call his doctor in … Redwood Point?"

"Yes, that's right," I said. "May I speak with Toby?"

She hesitated. "Well, he's not coherent right now, you know what that's like?"

"I understand. Is he restrained?"

Miss Smaridge came in. I ripped the sheet off my pad and gave it to her. She nodded. I'd warned her that something like this might happen.

"Yes, but he's not violent," Gray said.

"Can you hold the phone against his ear? I'd just like to let him know I'm coming out."

"Okay." To Toby, she said, "Would you like to talk to your dad?"

I heard some mumbled response then, "Dad!" He didn't sound like himself.

"Hi, buddy. Carly and I will be flying out there. We'll get there tonight or tomorrow morning. How are you doing, Toby?"

"Ty," he said.

"What?"

"T apostrophe Y. I've changed my name to that. Besides two. It's whipping."

"I'll be there as soon as I can. Dr. Gray will help you."

The psychiatrist came back on the line. She filled me in on what had happened and mentioned some medicine names and doses that sounded familiar. I told her I'd see her soon.

After I hung up, Miss Smaridge handed me a printout with the flight information. "I've emailed you the reservations and notified your sister by text. You'll have to hurry. The flight leaves at ten forty. Good luck, Garrett."

Jen pulled our car to the curb at the airport, and I kissed her goodbye. I paced on the sidewalk, waiting for Carly. *She will probably arrive at the last minute or maybe even miss the plane.* I shook my head.

Why did this have to happen now? Arthur could show up any second. I felt I couldn't relax until that was resolved. *Now I have something more on the stack. But I can deal with it.*

The California Redwood Coast-Humboldt County Airport, the oversized name designed to attract tourist dollars, was tiny. The airport is so small you can park and find yourself at one of the two gates in under a minute.

I got my boarding pass then resisted the temptation to go out to the sidewalk and watch for my twin. *If she misses the flight, no big deal.* The plan was for me to give Toby support and make decisions then have Aunt Carly take it from there. She was fine with that since she could do her writing anywhere.

I sat at the entrance of the TSA screening room and went over Louella's reports. *She's doing a good job, as usual.*

The TSA deadline came and went with no Carly. Of course. I passed through screening with three other people and boarded the small jet. I was squeezing my leather carry-on bag into the overhead when I noticed a lull in the background conversations and knew without looking that my movie-star-good-looks sister was on her way down the aisle. Sure enough, there she was in dark glasses, a body-hugging white skirt, and a tan silk blouse with more buttons undone than fastened. A tan laptop bag hung from her shoulder. She lifted her shades and gave me a wink.

"Where's your luggage?" I signed.

She looked down and up then dropped her jaw and put her hand over her mouth.

I took the window seat. "Ha ha. Where is it?"

She sat next to me and gave me a kiss on the cheek. "I guess I'll have to go shopping in Denver."

"They closed the TSA screening. How did you get through?"

She said, "No idea" but did a provocative shimmy that was borderline pornographic.

"Have you no shame?" I was half serious.

"You should try it. What's the latest with Toby?"

"Why were you late?"

"I was writing a good scene."

"Seriously?" I pointed to her laptop bag. "You can do that anywhere."

"I was on a roll. Sometimes the words just flow like magic. Toby?"

"Nothing new. Thanks for coming." I filled her in. The plane lifted off, and the cabin resonated with the deep roar of the engines, making it difficult to hear. No problem for signing.

"Do you think that by swooping in every time he's hospitalized, you are enabling Toby?" Carly asked.

I squinted. "You mean—what?—I'm enabling his illness? That I should let him deal with it himself or something? Tell him to just grow up?"

She crossed her arms and gave me a look that I knew from experience meant, *Just answer the question.*

"No," I said. "Absolutely not. This is mental illness."

"He's twenty-two."

"Doesn't matter. If he were just lazy or bad with money, I wouldn't be bailing him out like this. If it were Nicole who got into trouble, I would probably let her work it out herself. You don't actually think I should just tell him to get his act together and stop having episodes, do you?"

"I just wanted to see how you viewed it."

"Right." I watched the flight attendant work her way down the aisle, handing out snacks. I took a pack of pretzels.

Carly mouthed, "Thank you" when the attendant gave her a snack bag. Carly can talk but never does. She knows it sounds funny.

She then continued signing to me. "What does your swooping in accomplish?"

"Ah, jeez. He needs an advocate when he's in this situation. He can't take care of himself until he's better. You know that."

"Do you take Toby for granted?" Carly asked.

"No. What do you mean?" I felt as though I were being cross-examined by a badgering prosecutor.

She laughed. "How can you answer 'no' if you don't know what I meant? Do you realize what a neat guy he is?"

"You mean in spite of his issues?"

"His issues are irrelevant. And he lives his life to the fullest."

"Unlike me," I said. "Is that what you're saying?"

"He's happy."

"Oh, right. Yeah, he's happy when he isn't suicidal."

Carly opened her laptop and went to work.

The flight was uneventful, but I couldn't say the same of the drive from Denver to Fort Collins. She'd rented a Porsche Cayman and when I wasn't paying attention, had set things up so only she could drive it. Payback time.

When we got in the car, I looked behind the seats. "What if we need to drive somewhere with Toby? Where will he sit?"

Carly shrugged. "We'll cross that bridge when we come to it."

The accident wasn't completely her fault. On Interstate 25, we were fifteen MPH over the limit. A guy passing us in a Jeep was ogling Carly and failed to notice the Coors truck in front of him. He veered into our lane at the last second. If Carly hadn't been signing with me, she might have reacted in time.

We pulled over to the shoulder, the left front fender crushed, and the side-view mirror hanging off the expensive sports car. Carly was shaking.

I took a deep breath and got her to do the same.

Horny Jeep Guy apologized profusely, continued his ogling, and gave us a roll of duct tape that I used to reattach the side-view mirror.

After we exchanged insurance information and Carly had calmed down, I asked her if she wanted me to drive.

"No." She pointed at her chest, slid her finger down, then placed four fingers against her chin, and moved them into the palm of her left hand: *I'm good.*

She pulled back onto the highway.

"Three cheers," I said, "for the collision damage waiver." I'd insisted on it even though Carly was probably covered by her existing insurance and through her credit card company.

At the hospital, Dr. Gray explained that Toby was responding well to the medication. Lithium was part of the cocktail that Toby took for his condition, and it worked well. I was concerned because I'd read that if patients stop taking the drug, it is less effective when restarted. I asked the doc about it.

"I understand your concern, Mr. Goodlove, but a recent study showed that's rarely true. I'll send you the reference."

We learned that Toby had unwisely elected to hike the challenging Greyrock Summit Trail. A few hikers had called 911 describing someone who was pathologically talkative and had only a camera bag, inadequate clothing, and flip-flops. He'd spent the night on the mountain and was located in the morning by a search and rescue helicopter.

In his private room, Toby sat in a chair, reviewing photos on his tablet. The cozy space seemed nothing like a hospital room, with homey furniture and a window that looked out over the helipad.

Toby was a younger version of me, with thick brown hair that was just starting to recede in an M pattern. It begged for a haircut, something he neglected when off his meds. His scraggly beard reminded me of the one I'd experimented with when I was a teenager. Dressed in a set of green scrubs, he was happy to see us but, I was glad to note, not euphorically so.

We had a good time visiting. I watched his enthusiasm over the photos that had almost killed him. *I really have taken him for granted.*

When Carly stepped out to get something to eat, I asked about his text.

"Do you remember sending a text about a superpower?"

He thought for a second. "I don't remember that, but I know what I would have meant."

"Do I want to know?"

"Yeah," he said then paused. "Here it is: What do most people fear?"

I sat on the edge of the bed. "I don't know. Sharks? Tigers?"

"You're on the right track. They fear death."

I saw where he was headed. "Yeah, that's probably true."

"But I don't. I mostly like my life, at least when the medication is working, but I'm not worried about dying. That's the superpower that depression gives me. And you know what?"

"Toby, you—"

"I think you have that same superpower, don't you?"

It wasn't the first time I was amazed at Toby's perceptiveness.

"Maybe," I said. "I'm not sure I want to talk about this." I recalled my thoughts about sharks: I was less worried about getting killed than about losing an arm or leg.

"That's okay. And think about this: Normal people want, more than anything, to not die, but every single one of them is going to be shit outta luck. They're going to die. Boom. No matter what. But people who wish they were dead are one hundred percent going to get their wish. All they have to do is be patient."

Chapter Eight

LOUELLA SAT IN HER office. She brought up Google Translate on her laptop and plugged in her telephone headset. *Here we go.* Straining to remember her high school French, she said, *"L-homme parlez anglais? Une moment."*

"Pardon?"

She typed, *Is there someone there who speaks English* into Google Translate then laboriously read out the result, "Y a-t-il quelqu'un qui parle anglais?"

Some kind of grunt came over the headset.

Did they understand? She waited. It was one a.m. in Redwood Point and midmorning in Dijon, France. Louella smiled. *Maybe they take zee break to eat zee mustard.* Her kitten slept beside the laptop, and the coconut scent of her vape pen lingered in the air.

"Allo?"

Louella sat up straight. "Hello. Do you speak English?"

"Uh … very little bit." The voice was male and heavily accented. *Very leetle beet.*

"I am looking for Margaux Marchand."

"Margaux! *Oui.* Where she is?"

"Is she there?"

After a delay, he responded, *"Elle n'est pas là.* Margaux ... not here."

It took another twenty minutes for Louella to confirm it. Margaux had been scheduled to visit her relatives in France, but she'd never arrived. No one knew where she was.

In other words, Arthur wasn't the only one who'd gone missing. Louella sent an email to Garrett.

The next day, Louella found herself in Tommy's Joynt, a funky bar and restaurant in San Francisco. The place was dimly lit, and a wild variety of objects hung from the ceiling: skis, a trombone, Tiffany lamps, and more. Tommy's signature dishes included buffalo stew, turkey leg, and corned beef and cabbage. Louella checked her watch—4:35. *What the hell, I'll have an early dinner.*

The news article on Arthur's disappearance had done its job. Too well. They'd had to devote a lot of time to fielding bogus sightings of Arthur, something that annoyed Jen in particular. "We're a law firm, not a detective agency," she'd said more than once.

They hadn't hired any temps to handle the calls because Louella didn't trust them to distinguish valid sightings from those called in by kooks and well-meaning but misguided individuals. Many obviously worthless, such as the psychic who reported that Arthur was now an African-American, piloting a sailboat to South America. Another caller sounded reliable but had reported seeing Arthur in Jacksonville,

Florida, on the same date that he had been surfing with Garrett. It was the borderline calls Louella worried about. An inexperienced temp might reject the one sighting that would help them locate their missing man.

The call from a server at Tommy's Joynt not only sounded real but was confirmed by a coworker. Louella drove down and entered the restaurant armed with photos of both Arthur and Margaux.

Louella finished her buffalo stew, bussed the dishes, then located the servers who had reported seeing Arthur. She huddled with them at a back table. The men had both worked there for over twenty years.

The first server wore a red-checked chef's hat and had a black mustache that made him look like one of the Mario Brothers.

"That one doesn't look right," he said. The other server agreed.

But when Louella showed them the third photo, a shot of Arthur, they both exclaimed, "Yes."

The Mario Brother said, "That's him. He was really out of it."

"Excellent. Was he alone?"

They both shook their heads.

Checked Hat said, "He was with a woman. She ordered for him. He was like a zombie."

Louella pulled out the photos of Margaux. "This woman?"

"Wow! No, no," the shorter server had some kind of Spanish accent. "The woman he was with was very skinny."

Checked Hat nodded. "She was a whore. Probably from the Tenderloin."

"Do you know her name?"

"No."

"And when did you see them?"

"Two days ago. Late at night. Around midnight."

Louella spent some more time nailing down the particulars and getting a detailed description of the presumed prostitute. She thanked them, headed off, and booked a room. After a few hours of sleep, she hit the streets.

The Tenderloin district of San Francisco is downtown, nestled between some of the wealthiest areas of the city. Starting as far back as the Gold Rush, it's been the place to go for brothels, theaters, and all kinds of entertainment, both legal and otherwise. Light from neon signs gave a sickly glow to the trash and dark puddles of water in the gutter. Louella shook her head. *How could someone be in the mood for sex in a place like this?* Most of the people she saw looked sickly, too. She passed many tents made from cheap blue tarps.

Louella did more walking than the streetwalkers that night. Although she probably looked like a cop to them, she got plenty of cooperation. A few had even seen the news article about Arthur. None of them recognized the skinny prostitute from her description, which Louella admitted matched many of the pros she saw.

Around 2:30 in the morning, she got a hit. A sad hooker, who was obviously also a meth addict, recognized Arthur.

"Yeah, yeah. I seen him. He was with Fanny."

"Is Fanny a hooker? Really tall and skinny with long, bleach-blond hair?"

"Yeah, yeah. She's like the heart o' gold type, you know, and I think this guy—" she stabbed the photo a few times "—he was like her project or something. He was in, like a coma or something, you know? And she took him to her crib. She nursed him back to health, you know?"

"Do you know where Fanny lives?"

"I know where she used to live."

Louella gave the woman a twenty. "How about where she lives now?"

"Nah, I don't. I know someone who might."

Louella got more information, handed over another twenty and her business card, and called it a night. Back at her hotel, she turned out the light. *Tomorrow should do the trick, so to speak.*

Chapter Nine

A FEW DAYS AFTER returning from Denver, I read through my notes on a case that would normally have held my attention. A local entrepreneur had been caught red-handed shoplifting a pair of expensive headphones from the Target on the north side of town. The interesting aspect of the case was that he was a millionaire. In fact, he had a net worth in excess of seven million dollars. He'd been arrested three times in the past for similar offenses, and I'd gotten him off for all but one of those. This time, the video evidence was clear-cut. *What's wrong with him?*

Thinking about my son's issues and the disappearances of Arthur and Margaux, I found it hard to concentrate. I read entire pages without the words registering.

The intercom buzzed. "Garrett, I know you asked not to be disturbed, but I have an urgent call from Chinese Hospital."

I depressed the button. "A Chinese ... a hospital in China?"

"No, Mr. Goodlove"—Miss Smaridge's tone said she couldn't believe I was so dense—"Chinese Hospital in San Francisco."

I closed the case folder and tossed it on my desk. "Okay, put it through."

After the appropriate clicks on the line, I answered, "Garrett Goodlove."

"Hello, Mr. Goodlove. This is Dr. Christopher Powell at Chinese Hospital in San Francisco. We've admitted someone who has no identification but who had one of your business cards in his pocket."

I bolted upright. "Dr. Toll?"

He hesitated. "I'm Dr. *Powell*—"

"No, is the patient Dr. Arthur Toll?"

"Uh … I don't know. He's right here. I'll let you speak with him."

After a delay, I heard, "Hello? Am I speaking with Mr. Garrett Goodlove?"

I recognized his voice immediately. "Arthur! Where are you?" Stupid question. "Are you okay?"

"Is … is that my name?" The relief was obvious in his voice. "Arthur?"

"Yes. Yes! You're Dr. Arthur Toll. A scientist. So … what? You don't remember who you are?" I slapped my cheek. *Stop asking stupid questions.* "You've been missing for almost two weeks. Do you know what happened?"

"Thank God! As far as I can recall, I awoke in the meager residence of a kindly prostitute who goes by the name of Fanny." Arthur's voice became husky with emotion. "She says she found me in a state of unconsciousness on the street and took me to her home. Although I'm unclear on the exact timeframe, I eventually regained my faculties. As soon as I realized that I was suffering from memory loss of an extreme and singular nature, I asked Fanny to take me to the emergency room of the closest hospital. I cannot express to you my degree of desolation, both then and now."

"Don't worry, Arthur, we'll figure out what happened and make you well again. What *do* you remember?"

"What I have already recounted to you represents the sum total of my knowledge of my personal history. I must reiterate that, as you can imagine, I find my situation most upsetting and confusing. I confess I am not dealing with it very well. Who am I, Mr. Goodlove?"

Despite the apparent memory loss, he spoke with his same antiquated speech pattern.

"Arthur, you are a well-known scientist in the field of —" I paused. The irony was astounding, but perhaps it wasn't a coincidence. I decided to leave that for another time. No reason to add to his confusion "—neurology drugs. Please call me Garrett. We are friends. I live a few hundred miles north of where you are, and I will be coming down immediately. One of my colleagues, Ms. Louella Davis, is in San Francisco right now, and she may come to see you before I can get there. Do you understand that?"

"My powers of comprehension are intact. It is only my autobiographical powers of recall that are impaired."

"Good. Is Dr. Powell still there with you?"

"He is by my bedside, listening attentively."

"Please tell him that he may discuss your case with me then hand the phone back to him."

I heard the two men exchange a few words followed by the sound of the phone switching hands. "This is Dr. Powell. Can you tell me more about my patient?" Apparently, Dr. Powell had missed the news article about Arthur.

"Yes. His name is Dr. Arthur Toll, and he's a renowned neuropsychopharmacologist." I impressed myself by not stumbling over the word. "If you Google his name, you'll find that he is engaged in research on a drug that causes amnesia. He—"

"I hope this isn't some kind of elaborate joke, Mr. Goodlove."

"It is not. It's possible that his condition is related to his research. He works with a drug called propolofan, which induces amnesia in animal models of depression."

"Was he doing experiments on himself?"

"I doubt that. Let me think for a second." I held the phone against my chest, got up, and paced around a little bit, trying to get the gears in my brain to mesh. "Okay, sorry. I guess there's a remote possibility that someone injected him with the very drug he's been studying."

Dr. Powell hesitated, clearly skeptical. "This is unbelievable!"

"I realize that. Can you tell me what happened? From your perspective?"

"Yes. He's given me permission to talk with you. John Doe—sorry, Arthur Toll—came to the emergency room yesterday afternoon, complaining of a persistent headache and total memory loss. You're not a doctor, correct?"

"Correct. I'm Dr. Toll's lawyer. And friend."

"We had a psych workup done, which, apart from the professed retrograde amnesia, he passed. We noticed a particular ... antiquated manner of speech. Is that normal for him?"

"Yes. He was homeschooled by someone who taught him to speak that way."

"Good. An intern was joking that maybe he was a time traveler. Uh ... he presented dehydrated and malnourished. That was consistent with his being unconscious or semiconscious for several days. We expected to find head trauma, but there was none apparent. A tox screen was negative. A CAT scan of his brain showed some unexplained abnormalities, but those may have been incidental."

"What does that mean?" I asked.

"We're guessing they were there all along. We'll have to contact an expert to know if they are related to his amnesia. Do you know if he's ever had a brain scan before?"

"No, I don't."

"He's not suffering from anterograde amnesia—that means he doesn't forget things we tell him. It's only prior events he can't recall."

I asked, "If he had this drug, propolofan, in his system, would you be able to detect it?"

"I'd never heard of that drug before you mentioned it, but it's doubtful. The woman he was with when he was admitted said that she found him unconscious a week ago. Most drugs would be cleared out after that amount of time. There were no signs of regular drug use."

"If he'd been injected with something, would you be able to detect that?" I asked.

"I don't understand. I just told you—"

"No, I mean, would you see a mark at the injection site?"

"I see. Very unlikely."

"What if it was done roughly? Against his will."

"Still unlikely, but we will perform a thorough examination with that in mind."

"Did you find any bruising? Defensive wounds?"

"Let's see … he has a bruise on one elbow, but that would be consistent with a fall. By the way, he's become famous here, and everyone likes him."

"That's good. Maybe you'll be able to get his insurance information. I will personally guarantee payment for all procedures. If you wish to call in any specialists who could help, please do so. My private investigator is in the city searching for him, and I'll call her as soon as I get off the phone. I would like to have her guard him."

"He's in danger?"

"It's possible. He came to me concerned about his safety, then he disappeared. My investigator is Ms. Louella Davis. She's in her sixties and—"

"An older black woman with frizzy hair? Looks like The Oracle from *The Matrix*?"

I froze, blinking. "That's her. How—?"

He laughed. "She just came into the room, accompanied by one of our security officers. Just a second."

Overhearing their conversation, I learned that when Louella had arrived at the hospital saying she knew

Arthur, they'd allowed her to come up. I also heard my name in there.

Powell came back on the line. "She'd like to speak with you."

"Wait. Before you go. Please find out all you can about propolofan and Dr. Toll. I think it will help."

"I'm way ahead of you. Here's your PI."

"Hi, boss."

"I guess I beat you to him," I said.

"How'd you do it?"

"He had my business card in a pocket. The hospital called me."

"Right. Dumb luck. Don't give up your day job. I found the prostitute who found him on the street, and she told me she took him here to the ER. You want me to keep an eye on him?"

"Yes. I'll be there by morning. Try not to get kicked out."

"Kicked out?"

"When you vape."

"Funny."

"Let me talk to Arthur again," I said.

There was a delay, then Arthur said, "Thank you, Garrett."

"How are you doing, Arthur?"

"Better now, but still concerned, as you might well imagine."

"I understand. Hang in there. I'll see you tomorrow morning. Please give Dr. Powell permission to talk with Louella about your case."

"She's the African-American woman who looks like The Oracle in *The Matrix*?"

I frowned. "Wait. You remember the movie?"

"Sadly, no," he said. "I just heard Dr. Powell describe her in that fashion. I have no idea what it means."

"Okay, right. She has never met you, but she knows about you, and you can trust her."

"I will do that," he said.

"See you tomorrow, Arthur. Keep your chin up."

I traveled down to San Francisco and met with Arthur, Louella, and the doctors. Dr. Powell was convinced that Arthur had a true retrograde amnesia more comprehensive than any ever reported. He spoke with some of the scientists in Arthur's lab and concluded that he was indeed suffering from the effects of propolofan. He was already planning to submit a scientific paper on his case to the *Journal of Neuroscience*.

However, another doctor, whom Powell brought in from the UCSF hospital, disagreed. She thought Arthur was malingering—faking his memory loss. She asked if Arthur was a criminal. I assured her he was not.

Confident that Louella would keep Arthur safe while he underwent more tests in the hospital, I headed back to Redwood Point. The next morning, Jen insisted that I needed some time off and proposed an early morning bike ride through the redwoods. "Just what the doctor ordered," she said.

Fueled with caffeine, we loaded the bikes and started on the fifty-mile drive north to Prairie Creek Redwoods State Park. Jen drove.

When we'd almost reached the park, she asked, "So, you're sure he has amnesia?"

"Absolutely. Arthur doesn't have a deceptive neuron in his body."

"You've only known him a few days."

"It's enough," I said. "You'd feel the same way if you met him. Something he said was—how did he put it?—I am steadfast in following the tenets of Christianity, and I use them to guide my actions."

"But how could it possibly be? He doesn't remember his name, one of the first things you learn, but he knows what a hospital is. He knows how to use a telephone."

"Agreed. It's strange, but the brain is strange, too."

We stopped just inside the park. There's a bypass that travels seven miles through thick groves of old-growth redwoods, an area that's never been logged. It's paved and perfect for riding. I pulled my bike off the rack, a Specialized aluminum road bike. Even with our recent windfall, I couldn't justify a carbon-fiber bike.

Jen unloaded her Cannondale mountain bike. "You remember the story of Mario Bruneri?"

"Vaguely. An amnesiac in Italy? After World War I?"

"Right. I looked it up last night. It's a great story." Jen snugged her helmet onto her head and tightened the chin strap.

I got my own helmet on, locked the car, and we were off. Traffic on the bypass is sparse, so we could ride side by side and talk. First, we went across the wide meadow where a herd of Roosevelt Elk often grazed. It was empty, so apparently, they were on break. Then we passed into the forest. The trunks of redwoods put the columns of the Supreme Court Building to shame. Many were over a thousand years old, and I always made a point of looking up as we biked through them instead of concentrating on the road.

"What a magical place this is." Jen gestured toward the trees.

"Absolutely. Tell me the story."

"It happened in Turin, about ten years after World War I ended. A night watchman in a graveyard caught someone stealing a copper vase."

"In the graveyard?"

"Hush. Just listen. I'm not sure of the exact details." Jen rode around a chunk of redwood bark on the pavement. "The next day, the police found the guy wandering around, crying, saying he wanted to commit suicide, and claiming he had complete amnesia. He had no idea who he was. They put him in a mental institution, and I take it they were pretty brutal back then. That is where he stayed for a year."

"And his memory didn't come back."

"It did not. The doctors thought he had a mental block. After a year, a newspaper wrote a story about him and included a photograph. A woman named Giulia Canella saw the picture and yelled, 'That's my husband!'"

"Surprising she spoke English."

Jen rolled her eyes. "So, she called the hospital and arranged a meeting. For whatever reason, the doctors set it up so that the man and his wife would simply pass one another on a path on the grounds."

"They didn't say, 'Hey, we found your wife!'"

"Right. Anyway, he didn't show any sign that he recognized her."

"But she recognized him?"

A car came up behind us, and we got in single file. When it passed, Jen flared out into the lane again, and I came up on her right. It was the first car we'd seen, and when it was gone, it made the majestic silence of the forest more conspicuous.

She continued the story. "That's not entirely clear. Keep in mind that her husband had been missing for ten years. Since the war. The docs repeated the meetings, and after the third one, the husband and wife hugged. She broke into tears, and he seemed to recognize her. Finally, all were convinced that they'd solved the mystery of the man with no memory, and he went home with her."

"And they lived happily ever after."

"Not exactly," Jen said.

We came to the grueling part of the ride, and the story was forced into intermission as we stood on our pedals to get up the grade. My bike was lighter, but Jen's muscles were younger.

I joined her at the top, and we shared an energy bar.

"So why no happily ever after?" I asked.

"Because the newspaper recounted the remarkable tale and included a photograph of the joyous couple. A few days after that, the police got an anonymous tip that the man in the picture was not Mr. Canella but was, in fact, one Mario Bruneri, a criminal with a record as long as his *braccio*."

I looked at her. "Braccio?"

"Italian for 'arm.'"

"Show-off. Case closed?"

"You'd think so. But the woman refused to believe it wasn't her husband despite fingerprint evidence."

"She probably decided she loved this new guy even if he wasn't her husband. She didn't want him to go to jail," I said.

"Could be. The whole thing was bigger than the OJ trial, and court cases continued for years. The last one confirmed, by a vote of four to three, that the man was Mario Bruneri."

"He went to prison?"

She put her helmet back on. "No, the happy couple fled to Brazil."

"Where they lived happily ever after?"

"Probably." Jen hopped on her bike and started the downhill glide back to our car. I followed.

It was an excellent ride. We could honestly claim we'd ridden fourteen miles even though seven of them were downhill and no more strenuous than sitting on a padded fence rail. Back at the car, we took a blanket and spread it out in the meadow. We sat cross-legged, ate Egg McMuffins, and drank OJ. The sun was just warm enough to make it pleasant despite the cool breeze. We lay down together on our backs, watched the clouds, and listened to the whooshing of the wind in the trees.

"Are you appreciating this?" Jen asked.

"I am indeed." I took her hand.

"Someone told me it's a good idea to dwell on happy moments. Let them soak into your soul. It's good for you."

I chuckled. "It sounds like you've been talking to a Buddhist or something. Who told you that?"

"Louella Davis."

I got up on my elbow and looked at Jen. "Our Louella Davis?"

She smiled. "No. The other Louella Davis."

I smiled and kissed her then lay back down. A red-tailed hawk gave its piercing cry, and Jen pointed to it. I let the sun and the wonderful experience soak into my soul.

It felt good.

The doctors at Chinese Hospital poked, prodded, and scanned Arthur before releasing him. Louella emailed me the reports. The bottom line was that there was no way to know for sure if he really had amnesia or was faking it. The only objective result came from an MRI of his brain, but even that was inconclusive. I looked at the write-up: *Possible diffuse anomalous necrotic lesions in the dorsal CA1 region of the hippocampus; the basolateral amygdala; and the entorhinal, parietal, and posterior cingulate cortices.* The report included an image from the MRI, which, of course, meant nothing to me.

Louella drove Arthur back up to Redwood Point, and I insisted he stay in our guest room until we learned more. His car was nowhere to be found—Louella was working on that.

On the day of his return, I set up a meeting with his brother, followed by a trip to a hypnotist.

My telephone conversation with his brother puzzled me. First, Herman Toll spoke like a normal person— none of the antiquated verbal sophistication so characteristic of Arthur's speech. He didn't use the word "singular" at all and twice ended a sentence with a preposition. Second, his reaction when I told him we'd found his brother and that Arthur had amnesia wasn't quite what I'd expected. I'd anticipated *Oh, thank God.*

Amnesia? Oh no! His response was more like, *Oh, I see. Hmm.*

Herman lived in Willow Creek, an hour's drive from Redwood Point. Arthur and I got in the car and headed off. When we turned off 101 onto 299, I asked Arthur how he was feeling.

"I am beginning to think it improbable," he replied, "that I shall ever adjust to this singular situation. The two psychologists with whom I had intercourse at the hospital both believed I might expect to regain my memories, possibly through, at first, short flashes or images, followed by more comprehensive videos, if you will, of my previous life. One likened this process to putting together the pieces of a jigsaw puzzle, implying that as the full picture begins to take form, the process will accelerate."

"But you don't think that will happen?"

"I am doubtful. As yet, I have experienced precisely zero flashes of any kind."

"I'm sorry, Arthur. Maybe when you see your brother, it will awaken something in your mind."

"We can but hope."

Herman Toll lived in a converted barn that overlooked the Trinity River. When he opened the door, I didn't see an especially strong family resemblance. Arthur's nose was long with some ups and downs along the ridge between the forehead and the tip, while Herman's was a mini ski jump. Arthur had bushy eyebrows and brown hair on the sides of his head, while Herman's eyebrows were little more than shadows, and his hair was black and thick. Their mouths matched, however. Both were full, with a serious set to them.

I bowed a greeting, and Arthur extended his hand toward Herman, unaware that people didn't do that anymore.

"Here he is," I said, gesturing toward Arthur.

Herman stood there. "Here *who* is?"

I blinked and frowned. "Arthur. Your brother!"

Herman looked at Arthur. "I've never seen this man before in my life."

Chapter Ten

STARS DANCED IN MY vision, and I staggered to one side, hitting the open screen door. *How? What?* I craned my head back and checked the house number above the door. It was right.

"Wait a second." I took a breath. "Aren't you Herman Toll?"

He stood with crossed arms. Nodded.

Arthur chewed on his lower lip and showed no signs of recognition.

"Okay, hold on." I looked at Herman. "You're telling me that this man—"

Herman burst into laughter and clapped Arthur on the shoulder. "Man, Artie, you really had me going for a while." He shook his head. "I admit it. You are the master. Amnesia! And so elaborate." He pointed to me. "And this guy? This guy is great."

He turned to me. "You look just like a lawyer. Points off for his name, though, Artie. Goodlove? Really? I almost didn't catch on. So, you did disappear, that part was real, but then you took the news stories about amnesia and ran with it, right? You really are a genius, Artie! Come in, both of you." He went into the house, peals of uncontrollable laughter echoing in the large space.

Arthur turned to me. "He thinks it's just a joke."

"Apparently. When you were young, did you two—sorry. Never mind. In the lab, you'd mentioned that you liked practical jokes. I'm guessing you and he pulled those on one another."

Arthur shrugged.

"Let's go in and set him straight."

We caught up with Herman in the kitchen. It was really just a kitchen corner. The interior of the barn was one big room with exposed beams and cedar paneling everywhere. Herman had opened three bottles of locally brewed beer and sat at a table, drinking one. Arthur and I joined him. I snapped a business card down in front of Herman, moved my beer to one side, and opened my briefcase on the table.

"I appreciate a good practical joke, Mr. Toll, but I'm sorry to tell you that this is no joke. Your brother really does have amnesia."

Herman froze with his bottle halfway between his lips and the table. He looked at me sideways, not convinced.

I took out a manila folder that Ida had put together and slid it over to Herman. "These are some of the reports of the doctors and psychiatrists at the hospital in San Francisco."

Herman opened the folder and read through the write-ups. The blood drained from his face. "I thought

... I'm sorry, Artie. We used to play practical jokes. Oh, man."

It took a while for it to fully sink in. A few times, Herman asked questions that started with, *You really don't remember when ...*

"Mr. Toll, perhaps you can help Arthur fill in his history, even if you can't get him to remember it, and I'll leave you two alone to do that, but first, I have a question."

"You can call me Herman."

"Will do. Here's my question: Arthur has a distinctive way of speaking, but you don't seem to—"

"Right. He was homeschooled. I wasn't. I'm five years younger than Artie, and our parents decided public school was good enough for me. Be aware that I can, as this sentence illustrates, elect to speak in the manner to which you refer, but I made the choice, in the years of my youth, to eschew that manner of elocution."

"Got it." I looked at my watch. "I'll let you two get acquainted, but we need to leave here at eleven for our next appointment."

I sat out on Herman's deck. Willow Creek is far enough inland that it gets none of the fog we enjoy on the coast. The temperature had already risen to the eighties, and I was able to do something that wasn't practical at home: sit in the shade without a warm jacket. The river flowed past the house with a gentle rushing sound, and the air smelled different. Sweet. I think it was from the sugar pines that grew only in that warmer climate.

The two brothers were looking at old photos, and occasionally, shared laughter filtered out through the sliding screen door.

When we were leaving, Herman offered to have Arthur stay with him, but we deferred that decision until later.

Driving to the office of the hypnotist, I asked, "Did that trigger any memories?"

Arthur sat with his forehead against the passenger-side window. "I found that, in a sense, learning about my history, rather than lifting a weight off my shoulders, made more conspicuous the degree to which I've lost a sense of self. A sense of who I am—if that be reasonable to say. No, neither the stories Herman related nor the photos he presented sparked any flashes of recall. Had the stories and images been those of a complete stranger, our interview would have been no less provocative."

"I'm sorry, Arthur."

We took the exit for 101 south, and I tried to think of something to cheer him up. "Do you feel any … lighter without a history?"

"I'm sorry, Garrett, I'm failing to understand your point."

"You've learned about the nature of your research, right?"

"I worked with the amnesia drug with the hope that it can help those with depression."

"Exactly," I said. "The idea is that if patients can forget traumatic experiences from their past, their depression might be cured. You have no memory of your experiences, so—"

"Did my life story include scarring events? Herman mentioned none, but he might have been protecting me."

"No, none that I know of, though I think most people have some unpleasant memories they wish they could forget. I just wonder if having a total lack of emotional baggage could be seen as pleasant. You're understandably sad about having no memories, but maybe having no bad memories could be seen as a positive."

"I understand your point but have no way to evaluate it. I imagine you are suggesting I look at the positive, as they say. I—"

"Wait. You said, 'as they say.' But you can't remember —"

"Quite so, Garrett, but I suspect you shouldn't interpret that literally. Only as a figure of speech. Verbal muscle memory if you will."

"Yeah. My point is that many people think you'll be happier if you live in the present moment, neither reliving unpleasant memories from the past nor worrying about the future. You have one of those licked."

Arthur nodded. "I will keep that in mind, Garrett."

Our visit with the hypnotist was unproductive. He was unable to elicit any memories from Arthur.

Something is wrong! Louella felt it the second she stepped from her car.

She'd just returned from an amateur pool tournament and had parked in her driveway.

She didn't believe in any of that sixth sense nonsense. When people said they could tell if someone was watching them, she dismissed it. However, she was convinced that often subtle, subliminal clues might set off a sense of danger. Like the one she was feeling.

She looked around. *Can I find the subtle clue?* The lawn. At the edge, there was a place where the dew had been disturbed. Of course, it could have been a raccoon. Knowing that someone could be watching her, she stepped to the trunk and opened it. With the lid between her and the house, she pulled out her pistol. She checked that it was loaded, switched off the safety, and held it down by her leg.

Closing the trunk, she squatted down as if examining something on the license plate. She stayed that way for a full minute—*my muscles won't thank me for this tomorrow*—her eyes not on the car but on the house. *If someone's in there, he won't be able to resist looking out the window.* No, nothing. The problem with subtle, subliminal clues was that you couldn't rely on them.

She went to the side door, turned the knob, and pulled. It didn't budge. *Good.* It was still locked. On the other hand, it was unlikely someone would have gotten into the house through that door. The Segal lock was far superior to normal consumer locks, resistant to both jimmying and picking. She unlocked it and stepped into the house, the warning bells in her head quieter but still ringing.

Where's Lisbeth? Her kitten always met her at the door. Louella called out, "Lisbeth?"

Her high-pitched cry came from the living room, sounding more like a seagull than a cat. Was she stuck somewhere? It sounded like the time she'd climbed to the top of the closet door but had been unwilling to jump down. Lisbeth was bold and often got herself into sticky situations.

On full alert, Louella reached around and flicked up the light switch. Another cry came. Nothing else. She stepped around the corner.

A huge man with a full beard—like a lumberjack—sat in an armchair, his booted feet on an ottoman. He smiled.

"Well, Ms. Louella Davis, I'm guessing you'd be sad if anything happened to your pussycat." He picked up Lisbeth by one ear, and her rapid panicked cries filled the room.

Louella raised her gun and shot him in the shoulder.

Chapter Eleven

THE MAN DROPPED LISBETH, and the kitten, totally freaked from the sound of the gun, streaked off toward the laundry room.

Louella held her gun in both hands, aiming at the intruder's head. She could have drilled him between the eyes with her first shot, but she wanted him to live. She had questions.

"Move an inch, and you're dead," she yelled, louder than she'd intended. "Who sent you?"

Mr. Lumberjack was apparently too stunned to respond. He clawed at his shoulder, which was spurting blood onto the chair and rug in rhythmic pulses.

Louella kept the gun on him. *Must have hit an artery. Damn.* She wanted to check for a gun, but he was a huge man, and she was an old woman. Instead, she picked up her landline and dialed 911.

"I need an ambulance and police, right away." She gave her address. "Large man in his twenties or thirties. GSW to the shoulder, spurting blood. He was an intruder. I'm retired Detective Louella Davis, the homeowner. Please hurry." She laid the handset on the table.

Her house was only blocks from the Humboldt County Sheriff's Department, and the sirens began immediately. The man's face had gone white, his lips blue. His head lolled around, and his eyes rolled back.

Assuming the dispatch operator was still on the line, Louella yelled, "He's losing consciousness." She crossed the room. "I've unlocked my front door."

She moved toward the bad guy. Either he'd lost consciousness, or he was a good actor. If she didn't care about him staying alive, she would have just waited for the cops. Instead, still holding her gun, she checked him for a weapon and found a large revolver on the chair cushion between his legs. She felt his wrist then yelled out, "Rapid, thready pulse." *Not faking.*

Louella put the two guns on the floor and slid her finger into the bullet wound. She hoped she could feel the artery and squeeze it off. No go. *Come on, ambulance!* She pulled a doily from the back of the chair, balled it up, and pressed it against the wound, putting all her weight on it. *Don't you dare die, asshole.*

The crescendo of the siren told her the cops had driven onto her lawn, and seconds later, the front door opened. She turned, recognizing neither of the two officers, one man, one woman. Both had their guns drawn.

"We need EMTs," Louella said. "This guy is going to bleed out."

"On their way. Is anyone else in the house?"

"Probably not, but I don't know. Just my cat. There are two guns on the floor. Mine and his."

The policewoman kept her gun out while her partner went through the house. A backup team arrived, which included Detective Vince Rolewicz, her former partner.

The first patrolman came down the stairs. "Clear."

Next, two EMTs came in and took their bags over to Mr. Lumberjack. Louella stepped back and shook her arm, which had gone full pins and needles. "I'm too old for this shit, Vince."

"Let's go sit in the kitchen, and you can tell me what happened."

"I've got to find my cat first." She led the way back to the laundry room. "I just hope there isn't an open window or door. Lisbeth!"

Vince helped her look. "Here she is."

Lisbeth had wedged herself between the washer and dryer, too far back to reach. Louella kneeled and got her head down near the floor. "Come, Lisbeth. It's okay. Kitty, kitty."

"Should we ease her out with this broomstick?"

"No." Louella turned to him. "What are you, a dog person?"

"I wasn't going to whack her or anything. Have you got any tuna fish?"

"Cabinet to the right of the sink."

He came back in a few minutes with a plate. "I put some of her cat food on this too, and some cream."

"You're making me hungry." Louella put the dish down at the front of the gap between the washer and dryer. "C'mon, kitty."

Lisbeth didn't budge.

Louella turned around and sat with her back against the dryer. "Is the perp still out there?"

"No. He died, and they took him away. Your chair is ruined. Same for the rug, which is probably a good thing."

"What's good about it?"

"You've got way too much stuff in there. It looks like a fucking furniture warehouse." After a pause, he said, "You doing okay, Louella? You need a hug or something?"

"In your dreams."

"We need to go down to the station and take your statement."

"Yeah. I'm not leaving my cat. Get your notebook out."

Garrett would freak if he knew she was talking to the police without him present, but Louella knew it was a righteous shooting. She narrated her story in cop speak, and when Vince finished writing it down, he tilted his head toward the floor. Lisbeth was taking big bites of tuna fish. Louella reached over and petted her gently. Lisbeth growled while chewing. It sounded like *Nom, nom, nom.*

Louella shook her head. "I save your life, and you growl at me?"

Vince put away his notebook. "That's why I'm a dog person."

The day after Louella shot her intruder, I learned that, unsurprisingly, Arthur was a person of interest in Margaux's disappearance. His presence had been requested downtown, and he and I waited in an interrogation room. It had linoleum flooring from the fifties, a gray metal table, and stained acoustic tiles on the low ceiling.

"Am I correct in assuming, Garrett, that you've informed the authorities of my memory deficit?"

"I have. However, you have to realize that these aren't men of science. The sum total of their knowledge about amnesia probably comes from movies and television shows. Maybe some thriller books. In most of those, a character gets a bump on the head and loses his or her memory. Usually, the plot progresses as the character gradually regains his powers of recall. So that's what the police are going to expect. Either that or that you're faking."

"Can you convince them that my case is different?"

I shook my head. "Not today. Just be honest. If you don't remember something, just say that. Don't let their attitude annoy you. Stick to your guns. Tell the truth. Don't rush to answer questions in case I want to make an objection."

We sat quietly for a few minutes, surrounded by the musty scent of the old room and the quiet humming of the fluorescents. Finally, the door opened and in stepped my frenemy, Derek Slater. Slater the Waiter.

I shouldn't have been surprised. He was a police interrogator before he joined the DA's office. He wore a dark suit, and his blue tie was less flamboyant than the one he'd worn at the winery. Watching him drop down into his chair and slap a folder on the table, you wouldn't guess that he and I occasionally saw each other socially. It was as if we'd never met.

Slater placed a recording device on the table.

I pushed it back to him. "Sorry, Derek. No recording today."

"We record ... all our interviews," he said.

"Hey, lighten up. This is not a custodial interview, and a recording isn't required. We're happy to help you out, but Dr. Toll is free to leave at any time, and if you insist on recording, we're outta here. By the way, we could have met in your office. There's no need for this"—I waved my arm across the room—"intimidating environment. Dr. Toll has been through a lot, including spending some time in a coma on the streets of San Francisco."

"The detective on the case is out right now. That's one reason for the recording." Derek looked at his watch. "Maybe you can come back at—"

"No, Derek. We made time to come in and help. Ask your questions. Take all the notes you want. However, you're aware of Dr. Toll's amnesia, and I think you'll find that, to his regret, he won't be able to contribute much."

Derek gritted his teeth. "This amnesia business is the biggest load of crap I've ever seen in all my years as a prosecutor. I got to hand it to you, it's genius. How convenient to be able to say you don't remember as an answer to every question. I'm surprised you haven't thought that up before."

I took my time putting my briefcase on the table while mentally counting to ten. I opened it and pulled out a few sheets. I slid them to Derek. "Here are the intake notes from the hospital in San Francisco. You'll see that the doctors noted the amnesia as well as Dr. Toll's emaciation and dehydration."

"They didn't note the amnesia," Derek said.

"Yes, it's in the third paragraph."

"No. They didn't note amnesia, they noted that the patient *reported* amnesia."

"Well—"

"That's a very different thing, as even you must admit."

"Are you a doctor, Derek?" I stared him in the eyes. "I don't remember a degree in psychiatry among your many accomplishments."

"I'm no … veterinarian, but I—"

"Veterinarian? What?"

"—but I can recognize bullshit." He stabbed the reports.

I tried but failed to keep from laughing. Derek joined in. He had a way with words. Arthur watched, chewing on his lip.

"Okay, Derek, let's all take a breath and start thinking about what happened to Margaux Marchand. Remember, it was Louella who discovered that she was missing. Without her, we wouldn't even know. We're on the same side here."

He took my advice and pulled in a deep breath. He closed his eyes and tilted his head back. "That remains to be seen. Dr. Toll and Ms. Marchand disappeared at the same time. They worked at the same lab. But let me stay on this amnesia topic just a little longer."

He turned to Arthur. "Can you write? Do you remember how to read? You don't remember your name, but I'm guessing you can tell the difference between a rhinoceros and a giraffe. Is that right?"

"Well, I'm ... no veterinarian." Arthur delivered his line deadpan and with a perfect imitation of Slater the Waiter's tone of voice and hesitating style. It was the first I'd seen of his sense of humor. I've always felt that humor and intelligence go hand in hand, and his joke made me realize that this MD-PhD, who'd graduated at the top of his class at MIT, probably had an IQ that was off the charts.

Derek, stunned, opened his mouth—

"I sincerely apologize," Arthur said. "This is no time for flippancy; a young woman has disappeared."

Derek pounced. "How do you know she's young?"

"I told him," I said. "We've discussed this."

Arthur pulled on his ear. "Yes, Mr. Slater, I can read and write. I've experienced no difficulty with such actions, by which I mean they didn't need to be relearned. I can recognize animals. I can dress myself and even tie a tie. Although I haven't tried, I suspect I can ride a bicycle, assuming that was among my skills prior to the recent events. I suspect it was something I was capable of since I can imagine doing it. That is, I can almost feel in my muscles what it would be like— how I'd turn the handlebars to stay upright if I leaned to one side, for example. I know the expression, *It's just like riding a bike*, intended to convey that there are some skills which, once learned, are not forgotten."

I would have to talk to Arthur about volunteering more information than requested.

"But," he continued, "I don't remember who I am, and I don't remember things that happened to me. I cannot explain this paradox, and I don't know at present whether there are those, be they doctors, psychologists, or neurologists, who can."

My frenemy leaned forward. "When you say—"

"Derek, can we move on? None of us here are qualified to discuss the nature of amnesia."

"Dr. Toll," he said, "do you know anything about the disappearance of Ms. Margaux Marchand."

"I do not."

"Where were you during the week starting May ninth?"

"I'm sorry, I do not remember."

"What kind of relationship did you have with Ms. Marchand?"

"Same answer, I'm afraid."

"You don't remember," Derek said.

"Correct. I'm sorry."

"What do you know about the disappearance of Claude Debussy?"

"I'm sorry I don't know that person. I don't know anything about his disappearance, either. I assume it's a man."

"What about Michael Jackson?"

I said, "That's enough, Derek."

He stopped asking trick questions and apparently realized the futility of interrogating Arthur. Derek asked me about Margaux, and I described our surfing trip and my brief interaction with her in the lab, namely that she pinched my butt and said she was going to buy a surfboard. I also mentioned the abandon with which she ran around naked on the public beach.

* * *

I'd just gotten home when Slater called to tell me they'd located Margaux.

Five days earlier, a couple had gone for an early morning hike on the Lost Man Creek Trail. The trailhead was only a few miles south of Prairie Creek Redwoods. Dogs aren't allowed on the trail, but, as many do, the couple ignored the signs.

"Our dog is so well behaved that no one would object," they'd said. And they were right. Their fourteen-year-old German shepherd was mild mannered and expertly trained.

He was a retired cadaver dog.

Also known as "human remains detection dogs," these animals can perform at an accuracy of ninety-five percent and can detect the scent of a human body fifteen feet underground or thirty feet underwater. Most importantly for this situation, they can distinguish between human and nonhuman corpses.

The couple had hiked a mile when Indiana Bones started running back and forth along the edge of the trail then sprinted off into the redwoods, snapping the leash from the man's grasp. The shepherd didn't respond to their calls, something that had never happened before. After fifteen minutes, the man went in after it, guided by its barks. The woman waited on the trail.

After only a minute, the man cried out, *"Oh my God!"*

"Are you okay?" his wife yelled.

"Stay there."

When he and the dog returned, his face was pale. "There's a body in there. Parts of one, anyway." He leaned over and vomited. "It's horrific. Decomposed. Flies. Worms." He retched again.

Because there was no cell coverage on the trail, they had noted the location, hiked out, driven to where they had a signal, and called 911.

Soon after that, Inspector Granville called me and related what had happened. She asked that I come down and identify the body.

"Why me, Edith?" I said. "I only saw her twice."

"I'll meet you in the morgue in twenty minutes." She hung up.

I should have said no. The last body I'd had to identify was my first wife's, following her fatal car accident. I told Jen where I was going.

"No way, *koibito*," she said. "Let me call Edith back. She doesn't remember your history. I'm sure she can find someone else. Someone from the lab."

"No. I'm a grown man. I can handle this."

"You don't have to prove yourself."

"I'll be back soon."

"No," she said. "I'll drive you."

Anyone who's seen a crime show knows what a morgue looks like. The smell, however, is something that can't be conveyed on TV. Even with refrigeration and body bags, I had no trouble understanding how cadaver dogs could find buried remains. The scent of a dead human is dramatically different from that of any other animal. I'm guessing humans evolved a sensitivity to it since there's an adaptive value to avoiding places where dead people are found. *If cave smell like dead people, Ogg not go in. Ogg run away.*

Before I could stop her, Jen took Edith aside and told her about Raquel.

"That's okay, Garrett," the detective sergeant said. "I'll find someone else. This is just a pro forma thing anyway."

"No! Let's just get it over with. I can handle it."

When the coroner slid the tray out, the flashback was as vivid as it was unexpected. I saw Raquel even before he opened the body bag. My legs turned to rubber. I slapped my face, and the coroner gave me a funny look. He unzipped the bag, displaying only the badly decomposed head, both eyes missing and the jawbone exposed.

It was Margaux. Her telephone-cord locks spread around her. I nodded and closed my eyes. I wiped away some tears. The coroner probably thought I was in love with Margaux.

We followed Edith back to her office. When we sat, Jen took my hand.

Edith propped her cane against the wall. "She'd been partially eaten by wild animals. Probably a black bear, I'm told. The body parts were strewn around. She'd been left naked in a little clearing."

"Naked!"

"Yes."

"Cause of death?"

"We found a rope and some evidence indicated it had been around her neck. The body had some petechial hemorrhages." Edith consulted a paper on her desk. "The autopsy results have been delayed, but I expect it to be strangulation."

"Time of death?"

"We have a good feeling for that from her cell phone data. It stopped moving on May nine."

"So around the time Arthur disappeared."

"Yes."

"Why didn't you contact me as soon as you found the body?"

"The coroner wanted to cross some t's and dot some i's."

"For five days?" I asked.

"Yes."

"So you knew it was her, and you didn't contact us?"

"I'm sorry, Garrett. Your friend Derek wanted to do some more research first."

Chapter Twelve

I SAT READING IN the living room with no appetite for breakfast. My eyes were moving over the words, but my brain wasn't paying attention. I put the book down and stretched out on the couch, thinking I shouldn't have gotten out of bed.

Why hadn't I listened to Jen? It had been more than a week since my experience in the morgue, and I still hadn't shaken the funk that it had put me in. I'd been feeling pretty good, but when that slab rolled out from the wall, it sent me right back to the worst day of my life. In addition, things were turning south in Arthur's case. There were rumors that the police had discovered evidence that implicated him. Jen had hinted that it wasn't a good idea to have Arthur staying with us, that I was getting too personally involved, but I thought of him as a friend.

Laughter flowed in from the kitchen. *How can they be laughing at a time like this?* I shut my eyes, and my ears perked up when I heard my name. Their tone turned serious.

"… the most singular change in his affect over the last two days."

I didn't catch Jen's reply.

"… was since the start of that period which coincides with his viewing of Ms. Marchand's body, yet my understanding was that he had seen her but two times, during the surfing trip and once at my lab."

"You're correct, Arthur," Jen said, "but the visit to the morgue brought back unpleasant memories of his late wife. She and Garrett had a good but turbulent marriage."

"That is hard for me to imagine. I have been impressed to no small degree with both his equanimity and yours."

"His first wife was different from me, Arthur, and Garrett was younger and more … aggressive then. I don't think he'd mind if I told you the story. He and Raquel had had a serious argument, and she drove off angry. He'd wanted to apologize but couldn't get in touch with her. Then he got a call from the police telling him she'd been killed in a car accident caused by a drunk driver."

"And he had to go to the morgue to identify the body."

"Exactly."

"The same morgue at which he identified Ms. Marchand."

They stopped talking at that point. *Interesting that Jen thinks I'm less aggressive now.* I fell asleep. I dreamt there was a knock at the door.

When I woke, Jen was sitting on the coffee table, looking at me.

I rubbed my face. "Did something happen?"

She put her hand on my shoulder. "They arrested Arthur."

I sat up straight. "What? Why didn't you wake me?"

"I handled it. You're not the only lawyer in the house."

"For Margaux's murder? Did you tell him not to talk to anyone without one of us present?"

She nodded.

"Did you warn him about jailhouse snitches?"

"Of course. I told him one of us would meet with him after he's been processed."

I looked at the floor. "Damn!"

"Arthur handled it well. You'd warned him this might happen."

Louella sat at her desk, waiting until the appointed hour of two a.m., Ms. Lisbeth Salander asleep on her lap. Louella found she appreciated the kitten even more since she'd almost lost her, even if Lisbeth did growl at her when eating.

The police had been unable to identify the man who'd broken into her house. *Would have been nice to question him.* She didn't blame herself. Shooting him in the legs wouldn't have put him out of action. The shoulder had been the right call; it was just bad luck to hit the artery. Clearly, he was threatening her and wanted to force her to do something or not do something. Probably get her to stop investigating the Vanovax scam but not necessarily. She couldn't think of any other current cases that would result in a visit from such a man.

While waiting, she read over Margaux Marchand's autopsy report. There were two surprises: one major, one minor. The immediate cause of death was asphyxia due to ligature strangulation—no surprise there. The minor surprise related to numerous healed fractures and wounds. They suggested abuse but might have come from accidents sustained while engaging in extreme sports. Louella's contact in France called Margaux a *femme sauvage*, a wild woman. In any case, Arthur was off the hook for those injuries because Margaux had joined the lab on January 18, and the injuries predated that.

The major surprise: Margaux was pregnant. Eleven weeks along, so Arthur could be on the hook for that one. The DNA test was not back yet.

The clock downstairs struck two, and Louella said, "Okay, Google, be my French translator."

Her tablet replied, "Sure. Let's start," and both "Tap on the mic and start talking" and *"Touchez le microphone, puis commencez à parler."* Appeared on the screen.

She dialed her phone and put it on speaker.

"Oui, allo." It was spoken like one word. Weallo. The tablet displayed, "We are low," and *"Nous sommes bas."*

Louella chuckled. *It's not perfect.* She'd practiced using the app with a friend who spoke French, and it had done surprisingly well in general, not only translating out loud but detecting which language had been spoken.

It did better with her next sentence, speaking, *"Voici* Louella Davis. *Comment vas-tu aujourd'hui?"*

She described how the translator worked and explained that she was an investigator working on finding Margaux's killer.

The conversation went more smoothly than it had the last time they'd talked, and Louella learned that Oscar was Margaux's cousin. The family had been notified of her death, but Louella was breaking the news of the pregnancy. She interpreted the sounds that greeted that news as surprise but not shock.

"Do you know who the father might be?" Louella asked.

After the translation, the reply was immediate. "Not Stefan."

"Who is Stefan?"

"Stefan is Margaux's husband. Who is his server."

"I'm sorry," Louella said, "can you repeat that?"

"Stefan is Margaux's husband. They are separated."

"And you think that Stefan is not the father?"

"He is unlikely to be the father. They were not on good terms."

Louella asked, "And where is Stefan?"

"We do not know. We think he is in the United States. Maybe in the jail."

"Is Stefan a criminal?"

"He is a bad man. He is violent. Margaux should not have married him. We warned her."

The conversation continued for another thirty minutes, and Louella wrote down the information that might help her track down Stefan Moreau.

I'd been confident Arthur would be granted bail but groaned when I saw the judge assigned to the hearing.

Judge Ursula Love was tough. You might think her nickname, "Tough Love," was based solely on her name, but she earned it. No one would have thought it appropriate to call her "Sweet Love," "Tender Love," or, confusingly, "Good Love." She was tough, tough, tough, and she'd been that way even before she got breast cancer. Mostly, she was tough on defendants.

She'd been overweight for years but had lost thirty pounds when hospitalized for COVID-19 and never gained it back. With her weight loss, she had an anorexic-next-door look. The latest round of chemotherapy had stolen her hair, and she wore brightly colored gypsy scarfs to cover her baldness. When she smiled, she had a pleasant face, but I hadn't seen it in years.

I admired her strength of character, but I wished we'd gotten a different judge—anyone but her.

Our goal was to get Arthur out on bail. The argument for our side was that Arthur had no criminal history, not even a speeding ticket. Likewise, he was not a danger to public safety since he had no history of violence. On the other hand, Arthur had been charged with first-degree murder. Rope had been found at the scene, and Slater argued that its presence demonstrated premeditation. Bail is rarely granted in first-degree murder cases, but there was some wiggle room based on the strength of the evidence.

The last criterion for bail was related to flight risk. If Slater could convince the judge that Arthur had faked his amnesia, he'd argue that Arthur had already run away once. If I could convince her that the amnesia was real, possibly caused when the real murderer injected him with propolofan, we might win on that point. And of course, if the condition had been faked, why would he admit himself to the hospital?

After we'd gone through the preliminaries, I stood at the lectern. We were in Courtroom 4, with its cheap ceiling tiles, faded blue carpeting, and maple wainscoting. The faint buzzing of fluorescent lighting was noticeable only because it occasionally stopped. Jen and Arthur sat at the defense table.

I took a breath. "Your Honor, there are three reasons bail should be granted in this case. First, the basis for the special circumstance of premeditation rests solely on the presence of the rope. Mr. Slater argues that the murderer brought rope with him or her, intending to use it to strangle Ms. Marchand. But rope is the kind of equipment someone might bring when hiking miles into a forest. Many articles—"

"Your Honor." Slater stood.

Judge Love glared at him. "Sit down, Mr. Slater."

I turned back to the judge. "Many articles on hiking recommend taking along rope for emergencies." I paused, counting to five in my head. "Second, the penal code states that a defendant charged with an offense punishable with death cannot be admitted to bail when the proof of his or her guilt is evident or the presumption thereof great. My colleague and friend, Mr. Slater, has rushed to judgment here. We've just uncovered evidence that will provide much more than reasonable doubt that Arthur Toll committed this murder. The blood type of the victim's fetus excludes Dr. Toll as the father. In addition, we've discovered that Ms. Marchand is currently married, and that—"

"Hold on," the judge said. "Does her husband live in the area?"

"We don't yet know where he is."

"Is he the father of the child?"

"Also unknown. We are investigating, but we do know that her husband, a Mr. Stefan Moreau, has a history of violence. Not only that, but the documents I've provided show there's someone else with a clear motive to eliminate both Ms. Marchand and Dr. Toll. Given those discoveries, I doubt this trial will proceed, and at the least, they show that the presumption of Dr. Toll's guilt is far from great."

I looked back at Arthur. He'd been handling things well, considering he was accused of a crime that could lead to him being put to death.

"Third, Your Honor, Mr. Slater is suggesting that somehow Arthur Toll, an extremely intelligent individual, decided that the best way to disappear was to travel to San Francisco, lie in the gutter in a coma, be saved from death only through the actions of a kindly passerby, and then fake amnesia." I frowned as if confused. "If I understand his reasoning, Dr. Toll went through this ruse just in case he was found. I guess. Note also that he voluntarily entered a hospital. My question is this: Why didn't he just ... get on a plane and travel to a faraway location? He has a valid passport and enough money to fly out of the country. Is it just a weird coincidence that Dr. Toll, the head of a program researching an amnesia drug, is suffering from amnesia? If this goes to trial, we will show that someone injected Dr. Toll with the very amnesia drug he was researching.

"In summary, the prosecution overfiled when they presented this as a capital murder case. Dr. Toll is an eminent scientist with strong ties to the community, no criminal history, and no history of violence. He's been a model citizen all his life. The evidence against him is so lacking that the presumption of his guilt is weak."

I went back and sat between Jen and Arthur. He stared straight ahead but with a confident expression, as I'd instructed him to do.

The judge adjusted her scarf. "Mr. Slater?"

"Your Honor," he said, "Mr. Goodlove thinks it's reasonable … to take rope on a picnic, but in this case, the rope was thick and less than six feet in length. I have trouble imagining a practical use for such a short piece other than for strangling someone to death. As concerns the supposed amnesia, I am not proposing that it was part of Dr. Toll's plan from the start. Rather, I suspect that he, filled with remorse for the terrible crime he'd committed, drank himself into a coma. When he realized that his attempt to flee justice would fail, he came up with the genius plan to fake amnesia and, in that way, avoid all questioning."

There were several errors in his logic. I started to stand, but Judge Tough Love held out a hand to keep me in my seat.

"I am denying bail. I have not heard a good explanation for Dr. Toll's disappearance, and the danger it will be repeated is too great. There are a lot of mysteries here. If you indeed have new exculpatory evidence, Mr. Goodlove, I'm sure your client will not have to spend much time in jail."

She rapped her gavel.

Chapter Thirteen

IN THE PARKING LOT far above our favorite surf spot, Camel Rock, I watched Carly make the final steps of the steep, railroad-tie trail from the beach. Evidently not realizing I was watching, she dropped the boards on the grass, tilted her head toward the sky, closed her eyes, and let out a big exhale. Carrying just one board was hard enough, especially after a big-wave session like the one we'd gone through.

I felt bad about holding her to our bet, saying I'd carry my own board, but she shook her head. "You tricked me fair and square."

While I was watching her fasten the boards to her car, a guy with his wet suit halfway off came over to me.

"Great session, huh, dude?" He'd walked over from a truck with an Oregon license plate.

"The waves were a little big for me," I said.

"Hey, I gotta ask you. How do you get your wife to carry your board for you?"

I looked at him sideways. *Nice compliment.* People rarely thought I was Carly's husband since her looks put her far out of my league.

I smiled. "She's not my wife."

"Huh, but—"

"She's my servant." I was sure he'd just laugh at what was obviously a joke.

He didn't. "Wow, dude."

"I won her in a poker game."

He went back to his truck, shaking his head. *Probably an Oregon pothead.*

Carly was staring at me. She signed, "You won me in a poker game?" She's an outstanding lip-reader.

Back at Carly's, I got two bottles of beer from the fridge while she started the cold, damp procedure of caring for the wet suits. I handed her one then reclined like an Egyptian king on her chaise longue. She dropped the suits into a plastic tub, added a dash of Pau Pilau wet suit cleaner, and started filling it with water.

Holding both the hose and her beer in her left hand, she one-hand signed, "This is an intervention."

"Intervention?" I frowned.

She agitated the suits in the tub and nodded.

I sat up and looked back toward the house. "Don't you need, like, a group of friends and family for that?"

"I'm a proxy. For Jen, Nicole, and Louella."

Not sure what was going on, I waited. Carly pulled the wet suits from the tub, hung them on the clothesline, and started rinsing them with the hose.

I pointed. "You missed a spot."

She ignored me. She put the hose down and pulled up a patio chair. "Ready?"

"Ready for what?"

"I heard what happened after you went to the morgue."

"Oh, that," I said. "I've got things under control."

"No, you don't. Raquel and Patricia died six years ago. Yes, we both miss them every day, but we have to move on. You can't go back into depression every time something reminds you of them."

I said nothing.

"You need help," she said.

"I'm getting help. My doctor's given me medication."

"It's not cutting it. Has she suggested talk therapy?"

I started to get up from the chaise. "I don't want to—"

Carly pushed me back down.

"I'd rather be depressed than go talk to some stranger every week. Be *in therapy* like some Hollywood airhead? That's not who I am. Forget it."

"What if it wasn't a stranger?"

I narrowed my eyes. "Who, Quinton?" Quinton Lorenz was a shrink and a friend.

Carly made the sign for "no."

"Who?"

She took a breath. "Toby."

I frowned. "Really? Are you kidding? Talk about the blind leading the blind. His illness is worse than mine."

"Think about it. He's had talk therapy for years. I'm sure he's learned a lot during his many sessions."

"That's crazy talk. Just because I had a hemorrhoidectomy—"

Carly fingerspelled "TMI."

"—doesn't mean I can pick up a scalpel and do it on someone else."

Carly cocked an eyebrow. Smug. She was reading my mind with her twin sense. She knew I'd realized it was a pretty good idea.

Derek Slater sat behind his desk with crossed arms. "Admit it, Garrett, there's something wonky about this amnesia business."

I looked around the room.

He followed my gaze. "What?"

"You're sitting behind a Queen Anne desk in a kind of gilded throne-chair in a room with both a Persian and a smelly bearskin rug and old pictures of dead monarchs on the walls. I'm sorry, you were saying something about wonky?"

"Ha ha. Your client says he doesn't remember his name but can drive a car. Just admit—"

"Not that again. I admit that the brain is a strange thing. Can you explain hypnosis? Dreams? Is it wonky that you might remember your first kiss but forget what video you watched the night before? Or the name of someone you met five minutes ago?"

"What's your point?"

"You're making a judgment about Arthur Toll based on your personal conclusions about how the brain works, and you don't know any more about it than … Musty the Bear here." I stuck my shoe into the animal's open mouth.

"I've consulted an expert."

"The experts don't understand the brain."

Slater leaned back. "She thinks she does."

"Well, she's wrong, and you know I can get an expert to tell a jury why. We won't spare any expense on experts—"

"Where did Toll get his money?"

"Drug patents. If we get to dueling experts, you'll lose. Look, Derek, I don't fault you for making this arrest too quickly. A woman is killed, and the man who works with her disappears. It's a correlation that's hard to ignore, but it doesn't mean he killed her."

Slater said nothing.

"There was a New York City blackout a while ago. A woman in a high-rise just happened to plug in her toaster a split second before the lights went out all over the city. Of course, she thought she caused it. It's the way humans are wired."

"Oh, right. It's just a big coincidence."

"Okay, bad example. Here's a better one. People who have fewer friends die younger. Clear correlation. Those two things are linked. Does that mean you should try to get more friends so you'll live longer?"

"Some people have too many friends." He pointed at himself then at me.

I ignored him. "But consider someone who's morbidly obese and sick. Is he likely to have a lot of friends? No. How about a fit and trim runner? Will she have a lot of friends? More likely. So perhaps poor health causes both things: a lack of friends and an early death. Correlation doesn't mean causation. They disappeared *around* the same time. There could be plenty of other reasons for that. Maybe someone targeted them both."

"Good luck explaining that to a jury."

I watched him then continued, "I get it. You were worried he might disappear. If I were in your shoes, I'd have done the same thing. Arrested him. But the reasonable doubt is piling up." I counted on my fingers. "Unwanted pregnancy, father unknown. Violent husband. Old injuries suggesting abuse. Arthur's letter implying something might happen to him. Angry animal rights fanatics. And I can't even tell you about the biggest of all." I suspected Margaux was killed to prevent her from blowing the whistle on the vaccine scam.

"Why not?"

"Can't tell you that either. But any one of those things would—"

"Okay, okay." He held up his hands. "You made your point. I'll think about it."

"You'll just look stupid if—"

"Enough, Garrett! Stop kicking the bear and get out."

Pop! The champagne cork flew off into the woods. We'd assembled on Carly's patio for the celebration: Slater had dismissed the charges against Arthur. Apparently, he'd woken up and smelled the reasonable doubt. One of my rules is that all victories must be commemorated. The late afternoon sunlight filtered through the redwood trees.

It was a big crowd: Arthur, Jen, Carly, Carly's boyfriend, Nicole, Louella, and Toby, back from Denver. I poured champagne into all the glasses then raised mine.

I held it up. "Here's to liberty and justice for all."

Everyone cheered and drained their glasses.

Arthur leaned over to me. "I would like to make a toast if you think it suitable."

"Absolutely," I said. "Just a second." I opened another bottle and refilled the glasses. "Okay."

He raised his glass. "First, I should like to express, with this humble tribute, my gratitude for not only the stellar legal service which Garrett, Jen, and Nicole have provided on my behalf but for taking me under their wing and into their home as I've been recovering."

We all clapped, and Jen gave a little bow.

"Second," he continued, "it has disturbed me to no small degree, as one might imagine, that some, although none here today, have doubted the loss of my memory. I have no difficulty understanding their skepticism, and now that I have no reason, or at least less reason, to dissemble in this regard, I'd like to assure you that I indeed have a profound amnesia. Maybe it is unnecessary, bringing coals to Newcastle, if you will, to tell you this, but you can imagine my singular frustration at realizing such a statement, made when I could be presumed to have an ulterior motive for making it, was met with cynicism and doubt."

I clapped him gently on the shoulder.

"Third, and finally, I think—" he cleared his throat "—I think it would be appropriate if we take a moment, now that the dust has settled, to acknowledge the passing of Ms. Marchand. I, of course, don't remember her, but I understand that she was a friend of mine. I'm told that I was a religious man, so maybe we could hold her in our prayers." He raised his head and looked around. "I apologize for affecting the mood of this celebration, but I ..."

"That's okay, Arthur." I put my hand on his shoulder again. "That needed to be said. Thank you." After a brief moment of silence, I said, "The grilled chicken will be ready soon."

I didn't remind Arthur that the charges had been dismissed without prejudice. He could be arrested and charged again if new evidence arose or if the DA's office decided they could make a case. Double jeopardy doesn't attach until the jury is sworn in.

After mingling, I looked around for Toby. I found him on a patio chair a little ways into the woods, smoking. He gets extremely uncomfortable with groups of people. Even talking one-on-one is hard for him. He's okay with Nicole or me, but I'm always on the lookout for signs of uneasiness.

I sat on the redwood duff next to him. "How you doing, buddy?"

"I'm good," he said.

"I guess I can't get you to stop smoking."

"A therapist told me it's harder to quit than heroin." He tapped the ashes into a cereal bowl in his lap. "I have a theory about smokers. Some of them start when they're teenagers, to look cool, you know? Then they can't quit. But I think for others, it's an easy way to commit suicide."

I said nothing.

"They can't get up the nerve to jump off a cliff. They know that smoking will kill them, so lighting up is just a way to get their wish. Suicide on the installment plan."

"You think that's the case for you?" I asked.

"Nah. I got turned onto it at Sempervirens." Sempervirens was a local psychiatric hospital. "Did you know some places used to give out cigarettes to patients as rewards?"

"I've heard that."

We sat silently for a while, listening to party sounds and smelling the smoke from the grill and Toby's cigarette.

I said, "Did Carly tell you her plan?"

"Yeah."

"What do you think?"

"It's kind of the blind leading the blind."

I laughed. "That's what I said."

"It's worth a shot, I guess. I had one shrink that all he did was listen. He was a good listener, but he pretty much said nothing."

"Not even, 'How does that make you feel?'"

Toby laughed. We both had the same laugh. "Never. Just 'uh-huh' or 'I see.'"

"Do you think it helped?"

He shrugged. "Probably not."

Chapter Fourteen

THE NEXT DAY, LOUELLA told me some bad news about Margaux's husband: Stefan Moreau was in a Nevada prison, convicted of assaulting a prostitute. He'd put her in the hospital with a broken arm and a concussion. The news was bad from our point of view because he was behind bars when Margaux was murdered. So unless he'd hired someone to kill her, one of our avenues for reasonable doubt, if the DA refiled charges, was closed off.

Remembering that Arthur journaled much of his life in his lab notebooks, I suggested we go to the lab together and read through them. He'd moved back home the night of the party, feeling sufficiently reoriented to the world to be on his own. I reasoned that if someone had injected him to shut him up, it had been effective, so he was no longer in danger.

I picked him up at his home—one of those tiny houses—in Freshwater. He came out when I drove up and had a big smile on his face.

"I love my house!" he said. "I should like to give you a brief tour sometime and show you the many innovative features which make living in it a pleasure."

The house was about the size of a shipping container, with board-and-batten wood siding and white-framed windows.

"Does it feel like home?" I asked.

He thought for a second. "You know, it does, although I suspect that derives not from a stored memory but rather a general homey atmosphere, if that makes sense."

I nodded. "Why do you think you bought such a small house?"

"In conversation with my former lab partners, it seems that I spent most of my waking hours at work, so I imagine there would have been little to be gained by purchasing a larger dwelling."

At the lab, we were greeted by CEO Rita Vanhanna, who gave Arthur a warm welcome. She didn't say he could have his former job back, knowing it would take at least a decade of study for him to come up to speed, but she welcomed him to come work as an intern. All of Arthur's coworkers introduced themselves, doing a reasonable job of hiding their pity. The warmth of their feeling for their former boss was clear.

A chill ran down my spine when I caught sight of Henry Spiker, the man Louella suspected of running the vaccine scam. He was watching but didn't approach.

Before they took us to find the lab notebooks, Dr. Wagner, who was now the head of the program, asked if she could see the MRI scans from the hospital. I had them on my laptop, and we set up at her desk.

She scrolled through them then stiffened. "Oh my God! Wow, wow, wow! This is wonderful. Tom, come look at this."

Tom had a similar reaction. "Excellent. Show me the hippocampus."

She clicked through the sections and pointed with her pen. "No damage there."

"Arthur, do you have any problems with new memories?"

"I do not," he said. "Only with the recollection of events that preceded my disappearance."

"This is just like Markowitsch et al."

"Yes!" Dr. Wagner sounded like a female Arnold Schwarzenegger. "Check out the cell death here in the temporal poles of the prefrontal cortex. And note this temporoparietal lesion. Wow!"

I glanced at Arthur. He didn't seem to mind being spoken of as a lab specimen.

"Can you explain it to me in layman's terms?" I asked.

"Certainly." She didn't stop flipping through the images. "The lesions are what we would have predicted based on our animal studies."

"They show that Arthur received a dose of propolofan?"

She rocked her head back. "Well, we can't say that for sure, but the locations of the anomalies are in the areas you'd expect with someone with severe retrograde amnesia. In the absence of a head injury, the propolofan is certainly a possibility."

"You said something about Markowitsch?"

"Yes. That refers to a paper published in the *Journal of Neurology, Neurosurgery, and Psychiatry* in 1993 on a man who'd had a severe head injury. The man had amnesia in the personal-episodic domain—memory of things that happened to him—but less so for semantic memory —memory for words, numbers, etc. For example, the patient they studied knew exactly where Mount Kilimanjaro was but didn't remember that he himself had climbed it!" She pointed to the screen. "His brain damage was similar to what we see here. Is that clear?"

"Yes, thank you. Please send me a link to that article."

I forwarded her everything I'd received from the hospital and asked about the lab notebooks.

"Yes, of course." Dr. Wagner got up and led us into another room. "You can sign them out, but we'll need them back."

She opened a cabinet below a counter, and there they were: many brown leather notebooks, all labeled with a date range. I looked at the last one, and my heart sank. It was labeled "3/2021 - 4/2021." The last notebook, the one that might shed light on what had happened to Margaux, was missing.

I asked Dr. Wagner, "Where is the last one?"

"We don't know. We have searched the lab and have not found it. Arthur often took the current book home to record his observations. Have you looked in your house, Arthur?"

"Quite thoroughly," he said.

"Could it be hidden there?" I asked him.

He held out his hands, palms up. "I do not know, but I will search again with that assumption."

Dr. Wagner left us, probably to continue examining the brain scans, and Arthur and I each pulled out a notebook. The one I paged through included not only his scientific observations but notes about what happened in his personal life.

"What remarkable detail," Arthur said. "I wonder why I recorded so much of my extra-laboratory activities."

"At our first meeting, you told me you'd taken a vow to record everything faithfully."

He didn't seem to hear me, lost in reading his notebook.

He looked up. "I am going to start with the first one and read through all of them." He took a tissue from a container on the counter and wiped his eyes. "This will help me understand who I am."

I made a vow of my own: to find the missing notebook. Since Louella is good at finding things, I sent her a text asking her to help Arthur search for it in his house.

Louella hiked up the Lost Man Creek Trail, occasionally checking her phone for the GPS coordinates the crime scene investigators had given her. *Amazing that the phone can get that even when there's no coverage.*

The morning had been warming up, but then the rising air sucked fog and drizzle in from the ocean. She zipped her North Face jacket up to her chin and pulled her wool hat—the one her daughter knitted—down over her ears. Edith had planned to come with her but had been called away with a police emergency.

Just before losing cell coverage, Louella had gotten a text from Garrett: *Pls call me re searching Arthur's house.*

As she walked, she gazed up at the faraway canopy, almost obscured by the fog. *I should do this more often.* The trail was wide enough for a car, so she didn't need to watch where she stepped. When the GPS told her she'd gone far enough, she looked through the trees toward the right and moved her head around. *There. Yellow crime scene tape.*

Louella started down the steep slope, following the path that the crime scene investigators had made. She was tough but in a city way. She swore when she tripped on a root and once again when her orthopedic sneakers slipped off a stone when crossing the creek. She soon arrived at the clearing with wet feet.

It was almost magical: a clear area the size of a living room covered with duff—redwood needles, tiny redwood cones, and small branches made soft by the passage of time. She ducked under the tape like a fighter entering the ring and got a general feeling for the crime scene. It wasn't someplace you'd take someone to strangle them—you don't need a clearing for that—but it was a perfect spot for a private picnic.

Generally, the sheriff's deputies would have found all the evidence. In this case, however, bears and other animals had scattered both evidence and body parts. An animal might have picked something up and carried it miles away.

Louella acted as though someone had hidden a small prize and challenged her to find it. That had been her favorite game as a child. She selected a four-foot stick, and, starting at a corner of the rectangle formed by the crime scene tape, she began her grid search. Moving the stick side to side like a blind person with a white cane, she disturbed the forest floor material enough to uncover anything hidden beneath it. When she completed the search of the area within the tape, having come up empty, she sat and pulled out a granola bar.

After her break, she got up, groaning. *How soon before I need a cane like Edith's?* Her postbreak search took all afternoon, and she hit pay dirt just when she was ready to give up. Forty feet from the center of the crime scene, off in the woods, something manmade sat partially obscured behind a tree root. She took several photos of it with her camera as well as establishing shots to show where it lay with respect to the crime scene proper.

Kneeling next to it, with a stick the size of a pencil, she uncovered the object and transferred it to a plastic evidence bag. The item was something that had become popular soon after the COVID-19 pandemic hit the US: a pulse oximeter. About thirty bucks on Amazon, you clipped it on to your finger, and it told you the level of oxygen in your blood. Louella closed her eyes, thinking back to the article she'd read. People who tested positive for the virus but felt okay were sometimes sent home with an oximeter and told to contact their doctor if the reading got too low. Sometimes a dropping oxygen level was the first sign of upcoming problems. The device wasn't recommended for everyone. *Had Margaux tested positive for COVID?*

Louella held up the bag and examined the item. It was white and blue with an LED screen that was blank. The lid of the battery compartment was gone, as were the batteries. It looked as though it had been chewed on. There had been several rainstorms in the month since Margaux died, so fingerprints were unlikely. Louella spent another two hours searching for more evidence without success then fought her way through the underbrush to the trail.

Back in her car, she drove until she had cell coverage. Then she pulled over and called first Edith then Garrett and told them of her find.

Garrett asked, "What do you think that means?"

"Probably nothing important. Just something she had with her, or maybe it has nothing to do with Margaux. What's this about searching Arthur's house?"

"He had some kind of lab notebook slash journal that he wrote in, and we can't find it."

Louella waited for a pair of loud motorcycles to pass the turnout. "Are you having trouble controlling your overabundance of curiosity?"

"Uh … maybe."

"Have you talked with him about it?"

"Yes. He's expecting you, either today or tomorrow. He has a tiny house, so it should be quick to search."

She looked at her watch. "Okay, I'll go now."

At Arthur's, she talked with him for a while, and he showed her one of the other lab notebooks. The search didn't take long. There were no secret compartments, and she didn't find anything.

I sat in the La-Z-Boy in my home office, fully reclined. Toby sat behind me. The configuration was his idea, not because it was the stereotype of the psychiatric patient on a couch, but because it made him more comfortable.

Sitting face-to-face with someone, even his dad, made him uneasy.

Although I didn't allow smoking in our house, the room had acquired a tobacco odor from the residual smoke in his lungs. With the door closed, the study was quiet except for the occasional moan of Redwood Point's foghorn.

Toby cleared his throat. "So, uh … Mr. Goodlove, is it? What brings you in today?"

"Funny."

When he didn't say anything more, I twisted around and looked at him. "Hey, that's a special pen. Don't chew on it."

He put the pen on the desk. "Sorry."

I settled back and looked at the ceiling. "So, how is this going to work? Do I talk about my childhood?"

"Hey, who's the doctor here? Oh wait, I'm not a doctor."

"C'mon, Toby, be serious. I'm asking you how it will work."

He took a breath. "Okay, I'm going to act like I have a plan, and here it is. I'm going to do what helped me. From a real shrink. What he did was give me some coping things. Coping strategies, you know? First, why don't you tell me what the problem is? How you see it."

"Okay. It's pretty simple. I know how lucky I am—"

"You mean 'cause of your wonderful son."

"Wonderful son?"

"Ha ha. Now, who's not being serious?"

I scratched my ear. "I know I'm lucky, but sometimes things seem hopeless. It's crazy."

"I'd prefer that you not use that term, Mr. Goodlove."

"But the worst is that when something reminds me of … of the death of Raquel or the death of Patricia, it really knocks me down." I realized then that talking with a stranger might have been easier than telling this to my son.

"So, when something bad happens, you get depressed."

"Right."

"For just a day or two?" he asked.

"More like a week. It varies."

"Let me tell you a story." He paused. "Once upon a time, there was a kingdom where everyone walked barefoot. One day, the queen stepped on a rock and cut her foot. When she got back to the castle, she decreed that all the streets must be covered with leather so that could never happen again. Her jester said, 'Or maybe you could, like, just wear leather shoes. Duh.' So, she had him beheaded."

"Okay, good point. One can't expect a world in which nothing bad happens. You need to change the way you react to bad experiences. But that's just like saying, 'You can't let things bother you.' Easier said than done."

"Well, I'm going to teach you some hacks to do that, Dad."

It was probably the placebo effect, but ten days after Toby and I started our sessions, I was feeling a little better about life. In addition to the psychological hacks he was teaching me, it felt good to reconnect with him. I'm not sure we'd ever had such intimate conversations. But I was about to have my new emotional resilience tested.

Jen knocked on the door of my study while Toby and I were having a session. She came in. It was after dinner, around eight.

"Jen, we need—"

"I know, but this is important." She handed me the phone.

"Hello?"

"Hello, Garrett. This is Arthur. I'm sorry to have to tell you that I have once again been arrested. I have said nothing to anyone and told them right away that I wanted my lawyer."

"Okay." I held the phone against my chest for a second and heaved a sigh that would have been dispiriting for Arthur to hear. I put it back against my ear. "Okay, I'm coming right over. Hang in there."

I stood. "I've gotta go, Toby."

"No fortune-telling, Dad."

"Uh, right." I went to change my clothes. One of the tricks he'd taught me was to avoid the "cognitive distortion" in which one predicts a bad outcome without realistically evaluating the actual chances of that outcome. It's true I had already imagined my client and new friend receiving a lethal injection. *No, that's unlikely. Isn't it?*

I phoned Derek. "What's the story?"

"Simple. We found your client's DNA on the murder weapon." The smugness in his voice put my teeth on edge. "This will be an open-and-shut case."

"We'll see about that." I hung up.

At the jail, I couldn't do much more than offer moral support. Arthur was handling it pretty well, perhaps because he'd already gone through it once and knew what to expect.

This time we had a stroke of luck. Judge Tough Love was ill following a chemo treatment. At the arraignment, Judge Swanson listened to my arguments and set bail at one million dollars. The next day, Arthur was free.

I learned that through a wet-vacuum-based collection method, DNA had been extracted from tiny skin cells on the rope. It matched Arthur's DNA. Unless we could find a way to knock that down, it looked like we'd be going to trial.

Chapter Fifteen

MOST PEOPLE DON'T REALIZE how long it takes to prepare for a murder trial. Arthur was charged in June, and the trial wouldn't start until October. The US Constitution states that, "In all criminal prosecutions, the accused shall enjoy the right to a speedy and public trial" but doesn't specify the meaning of "speedy." California defines it as sixty days, but Arthur, like most defendants, waived that.

In mid-July, Jen and I waited for Nicole to come into my office for our weekly status meeting. Jen gave me a long kiss on the cheek.

I frowned. "What was that for?"

"Complaining?"

"You know I'm not."

"Thank you for taking charge of your ... moods, working hard to get things under control."

I'd resumed pulling my weight in the firm, taking more cases and less time off.

"Carly and Toby deserve a lot of the credit," I said.

Carly for suggesting my sessions with Dr. Goodlove, and Toby for doing a passable imitation of a real shrink. He and I got together about twice a week, and in addition to his secondhand coping strategies, I think I benefited simply by hanging out with my son.

Nicole bustled in right on time and dropped a pile of papers on the small conference table without looking up.

"Something wrong?" I asked.

"It's the polygraph evidence."

A polygraph test is generally admissible only if all parties agree to it, but our situation was different.

Nicole continued, "I've been talking with Slater's office, and I can't get them to understand that we're not using it as a lie detector."

"In a sense, we are. We're showing that Arthur isn't lying about having amnesia."

"Seriously, Dad? You don't get it either?"

"No, I do. We're not using it directly for—"

She put up a hand and took a breath. "Okay, I'll put it to you the same way I'll lay it out in the motion. We used the polygraph not to see if Arthur was lying, but to see if his body reacted differently to photos of celebrities versus random, unknown people. It did not. For example, he had the same response when shown a photo of Abraham Lincoln versus a photo of some random person with similar characteristics. He never displayed what the scientists call a 'recognition response.'"

"That's a nuance that might be lost on the judge," I said. "This is what Slater will say when he argues against the motion." I stood and leaned forward a little, the way Slater stands, and imitated his William Shatner speaking affectation. "But … let's say the doctor … puts up a picture and says, 'Do you … recognize this man?' The polygraph would be used to see if Arthur was lying when he said he didn't. How is that different … from what the defense is saying?"

Jen laughed at my impression.

Nicole smiled then fluttered her lips. "But it is different. You see that, right?"

"I do, but I'm not sure it's different enough to force it to be admissible. The problem with a lie detector test is that it isn't reliable. You can go on the internet to learn how to cheat. Things like biting your tongue really hard at the right time. Slater will say that Arthur cheated somehow, and that's why the machine didn't detect his reactions to famous faces."

Nicole crossed her arms. "But the scientist will say that's much harder to do."

"And Slater will get another scientist to say it's not."

Jen said, "But we should try anyway. It's all we have, really, to objectively show that he's not faking it."

Nicole and I both agreed.

Jen paged through her notes. "Luckily, our case doesn't depend on that, but it will help if the jury doesn't think he's trying to scam everyone."

The elephant in the office was Arthur's DNA on the rope, but we were avoiding that for the time being.

"Okay," I said. "What about the security cam footage?" A security camera in Orick had captured Arthur's car traveling south on the afternoon of the murder.

Jeri shook her head. "Common car. Can't see the occupants or the plate. And why wasn't it seen traveling north? I don't see that as a problem."

"And his car hasn't shown up anywhere?" Nicole asked.

"No," I said. "That's surprising, but I'm not sure it will influence the case."

Nicole tapped a finger on the table. "I don't agree. If he were trying to get away, he'd take steps to make the car disappear. It fits the prosecution's narrative."

"But we can argue that—wait a second …" I searched for the idea my subconscious was trying to send me.

"Earth calling Dad."

I got it. "I've got an idea for the polygraph stuff. The scientist who did the test, he isn't a polygraph expert, right?"

"No. He's a respected psychologist in the field of memory research."

"Okay, perfect. Here's my idea. Instead of presenting this as a polygraph test, instead of even saying the word 'polygraph,' we—"

Ida knocked on the door and came in.

"Ida, we're still in the middle of—"

"I have the chief of police of Monterey on the line. He says it's urgent."

A chill went through me. Toby was on a shoot in Big Sur. *Not again.*

I pushed a button on the phone and put the receiver to my ear. "This is Garrett Goodlove."

"You're Mr. Garrett Goodlove."

"Yes, that's right."

"You're the father of Toby Goodlove?"

I squeezed my fist, digging my fingernails into my palm. This felt worse than the other times since our sessions had brought Toby and me closer than ever before.

"Yes," I said.

"I'm afraid I have some bad news for you, sir …"

"Yes?"

"I'm sorry to tell you that your son is dead."

"No, no, I just saw him two days ago."

"I'm very sorry, sir."

Nicole came over and put her head next to mine so she could hear both sides of the conversation.

A begging tone crept into my voice. "Toby is tall with a scraggly beard and dark brown hair. Could it be someone else who had his identification?"

"No, sir," the chief said. "It is Toby who is dead. I'm —"

"Suicide?"

"What?"

"Did he commit suicide?"

"Oh, I see. No, not at all. Your son is a hero, although I wouldn't recommend that anyone do what he did."

I said nothing.

"An escaped prisoner held a pistol to a woman's head. In her mouth, actually. A mother with three young children. There was a standoff. Our sniper couldn't shoot because of the danger the criminal's pistol would go off. Your son went up to the perp and said something to him. The man turned the gun on Toby, and our sniper shot the man. Unfortunately, the perp got his shot off before he went down. That shot killed your son. The

EMTs did everything they could, but they couldn't save him. I'm sorry."

I stared straight ahead and handed the phone to Jen.

Carly, Nicole, and I sat together in my living room, mostly just being together without talking. I know the term "misery loves company" refers to something completely different, but it was true that it helped to share our grief. Like a support group. I told them how Toby had said he wasn't afraid of death. I'm not sure that helped any.

Jen stayed nearby and handled the necessary phone conversations with the police, the Monterey morgue, and a funeral home. She brought us food and coffee, but we didn't touch it. Zach, Carly's boyfriend, stopped by to offer his condolences.

Nicole and Carly slept in our guest room. Around four in the morning, unable to shut my mind down, I got up and wandered around. Then, like someone unable to keep from probing a sore tooth with his tongue, I went to my computer and searched for videos of the event on YouTube. I found several uploads from people who'd filmed the whole thing.

There was my son, walking up to the killer as if there were nothing to fear. A voice over a megaphone—certainly the police—told him to stop, but he ignored it. They couldn't send any officers in to grab him without possibly provoking the gunman. Toby stepped right up to the killer and said something. The video ended. I watched it again. *I can see his lips move, but—*

I put my tablet down and went into the guest room. I shook Carly's shoulder. She's a deep sleeper, but she woke, figured out where she was, and came back with me into the living room, rubbing her eyes.

I signed, "I have a video of Toby when he went to the gunman. I can see his lips when he talks, but—"

"No," she replied.

"What?"

"I won't tell you what he said."

I frowned at her.

"I've already seen it," she said.

"So you know what he said."

She clenched her teeth.

"You have to tell me. I have a right to know. Please, Carly."

I saw her jaw muscles working as she stood there with her thousand-yard stare. Deciding. Then she hugged me. That told me what I didn't want to know. I sobbed a few times, and she hugged me harder.

When we broke the hug, I looked in her eyes. "Tell me the words."

"Toby said, 'Shoot me instead. You'll be doing me a favor.'"

Toby had committed suicide after all. He'd seen an opportunity, and he took it.

Chapter Sixteen

IN MID-AUGUST, A month after Toby died, my mental state was still on a downward trajectory. Nicole and Carly seemed to deal with it better than I, but I was closer to him than they were, especially after our psychotherapy sessions. The coping strategies he'd taught me weren't up to handling such a monster of a mental crisis. It was like using a slingshot against King Kong.

Arthur's trial was two months away, and I was slogging, robot-like, through the drudgery of preparing for it. How could we prevail if the spark of creativity that helped me come up with innovative litigation strategies had been drenched with cold water?

I was staring out the window at the dreary weather when the intercom came to life.

"Garrett, your ten o'clock is here. Arthur Toll."

Damn. I'd forgotten. "Please give me five minutes, Ida, then send him in."

I slapped my cheeks and took a deep breath. *Don't infect him with your low spirits.* I sat at my desk and brought up the evidence summary on my laptop.

Arthur came in, and we bowed to each other. Bowing just didn't have the same impact as shaking hands. There's something primal about physical touch, apparently.

"Garrett, I would like to convey, once again, my deep sorrow at the loss of your son."

"Thank you, Arthur."

He paused, probably wanting to put distance between his offer of sympathy and the mundane reason for his visit, if you can call being accused of murder mundane.

He cleared his throat. "I have perused, several times over, the materials you sent me which outline the evidence against me. Based on those data, I have come to the obvious conclusion that it was I who murdered Ms. Marchand."

"Well, you're not a lawyer, are you?" My words dripped with venom.

I'm not sure which of us was more stunned. Arthur's eyes widened, and his eyebrows bunched up.

I leaned forward. "Oh, Arthur, please forgive me. I'm going through a rough time, and I—"

"It's okay, Garrett. I under—"

"No, it's not. It's not okay as a friend and especially not okay as your attorney. I hope you will be able to forgive me. Please give me a second to gather my thoughts, and I will explain why the situation isn't as dire as it seems."

I closed my eyes and took some cleansing breaths—one of the touchy-feely things that Toby had taught me. Not sure it helped.

I opened my eyes to find Arthur staring at me.

I said, "I was remiss in sending you those things without explanation. That's another example of how my grief—and I don't see this as a valid excuse—has been influencing my work. It may be better if I turn things over to—"

"No, Garrett. I want you."

"Thank you. Let's go over some of the evidence, but first, I'd like to say that we've spent no small amount of time together, as you'd say, since your reappearance. There is simply no way that the person I've come to know would kill someone."

"But what if I was a different person before?"

I shook my head. "It's true that I only knew you for a few days before the murder, but everything I saw confirms that you are the same decent, honorable man I've come to know since."

Arthur just stared at me.

"What?" I said.

"It was but a few seconds ago that you snapped at me. You spoke in a manner which deviated substantially from the tone to which I've become accustomed. While I appreciate the stress under which you've found yourself and understand why you might speak that way, it illustrates the degree to which anyone might act out of character. Might it be true that some great emotion compelled me to act in an uncharacteristic fashion?"

"Tie a rope around a woman's neck and strangle her?"

He took a deep breath then nodded. "I agree that seems unlikely. Could it be the case, however, that a jury, not knowing me, might believe such a radical transformation had occurred?"

"Dr. Jekyll and Mr. Hyde."

"Pardon me?"

"Sorry, never mind that," I said. "We will find some way to counter that possibility."

"I presuppose you do not wish to put me on the stand."

"That's right. Do you know why?"

"In addition to studying my lab notebooks, I have been reading up on legal issues. Thus, I know that under the Fifth Amendment, and as further codified by section nine thirty of California's evidence code, and I quote, 'a defendant in a criminal case has a privilege not to be called as a witness and not to testify.'"

It was easy, since Arthur had less knowledge of the world than a five-year-old, to forget his extraordinary intelligence. I also learned that he was a speed-reader and a sponge for knowledge.

"As to your question," he said, "I can envisage at least two problems with my taking the stand. First, in the brief period since this began, I've recognized that my singular manner of speech leads new acquaintances to presume I feel superior to them. Such a view, in the mind of a juror, would be disadvantageous. Second, upon cross-examination, the prosecutor might appear to trip me up, if you will, regarding my contention that I have retrograde amnesia. As an example, if I mention something I've learned since the event, the prosecutor will undoubtedly seize upon it as evidence that my amnesia is counterfeit."

"Exactly right."

"If I may bring us back to the fear I mentioned, the two most injurious pieces of evidence are, in my estimation, the lack of defensive wounds and the presence of my DNA on the rope. Those things, taken together, seem damning."

"I understand," I said. I explained several different ways we could defuse those things and went over our strategies for handling other damaging evidence as well. In the end, I'm not sure I convinced Arthur of his own innocence. *If I can't do that, how can I persuade twelve jurors?*

Whistling the ungrammatical "Me and Julio Down by the Schoolyard," I flipped the Swedish pancake into the air. And froze. The crepe-like pancake landed on the edge of the omelet pan. One half broke away and landed on the floor.

I was whistling! When was the last time that happened? Not once in the two months since Toby had died, certainly. I didn't want to think about it too much. Obsessing over my thoughts was one of the things he'd taught me to avoid, and I didn't want to jinx anything, but maybe I'd turned a corner.

I finished cooking the half pancake, cleaned up the mess on the floor, and added batter to the pan for another. The warm kitchen smelled like a bakery. Rain from the first storm of the season showered against the counter-to-ceiling windows.

Jen came in, half asleep, wearing her white robe.

"I feel good," I said.

That woke her up. She came over and gave me a hug. "I knew that you would."

I laughed. "Did you say that on purpose?"

She chuckled and nodded against my chest.

"James Brown?"

She nodded again then leaned back and looked up at me. "But I'm serious. You were making such good progress before Toby passed. Whatever he was teaching you seemed to be working. I was pretty sure you'd weather this."

"I'm not out of the woods yet." But I did feel different.

Toby had explained that one could rewire one's brain by paying more attention to good things. *Could my brain be slightly different now?* Toby's death ranked behind Raquel's, but—*Stop!* One of the things Toby had taught me was to call a halt when I veered toward negative thoughts.

We sat down to eat, rolling up the pancakes with jelly inside. I finished mine and drank coffee from my "World's Best Lawyer" mug. The one Nicole had given me.

I put the mug down. "I've got some new ideas on the case."

"It's only ten days away."

"I don't believe Spiker's alibi." The story of the vaccine fraud had hit the papers even though the FBI hadn't finished its investigation. Dr. Spiker, before being exposed, had a perfect motive to get rid of both Arthur and Margaux. The problem was that he had a strong alibi.

Jen said, "The woman first said Spiker wasn't with her but then admitted he was. That makes the alibi more convincing."

"And did her husband divorce her?" I asked.

"I don't know, did he?"

"No, he didn't."

"Affairs don't always result in divorces."

"I'm going to have Louella look into it some more. Remember, Spiker's smart. And I want to put more effort into finding Arthur's lab notebook."

Jen scoffed. "Not that again. I can't imagine he wrote down that he didn't kill Margaux or something like that. Even if he did, it's not going to convince anyone." She jumped when a gust of wind rattled rain against the windowpanes.

"Well, let's say he wrote that he went to, say, Sonoma on the day of the murder. We could maybe find some security camera footage that shows him there. Maybe *he* has an excellent alibi that he forgot."

"He wrote stuff like that in the lab notebook?"

"He did. He was a little obsessive about it."

"Well, that's fine," Jen said, "but if Louella hasn't found it by now, I'm guessing it's lost for good."

We had two final motions to argue before the trial got underway.

The first concerned Arthur's letter. It was an important part of our defense, and to bring it into evidence, we had to lay a foundation for it. Whenever something tangible is presented, evidence "sufficient to support a finding that the item is what the proponent claims it is" must be given. For example, you can't enter a video into evidence until you can demonstrate where it came from.

I was the foundation for Arthur's letter. That is, I needed to say, "Arthur gave me this letter." Simple. There are, however, rules against a lawyer testifying in a trial in which he is the advocate. The danger is that the jury might assign too much or too little weight to what he says. But we met the exceptions to that rule. Namely, the origin of the letter was uncontested, and we'd gotten written consent from Arthur to present it.

With several days to go before jury selection, we found ourselves in Courtroom 2, looking up at Judge Ursula "Tough" Love. Her assignment to our trial was a bad thing, but my rewired brain felt we could deal with it. I avoided falling into the trap of fortune-telling, thinking all was lost. I kept telling myself that she was tough but fair.

Health-wise, she looked neither better nor worse than she had back in June at the first bail hearing, due in part to expertly applied makeup. Rumor had it that she was losing the battle against her cancer.

Humboldt County courtrooms had none of the grandeur of those in the movies. Courtroom 2 was the smallest and resembled a theater in a multiplex cinema —the one for the less popular movies. The harsh fluorescent lighting was set into the acoustic ceiling tiles, and a blackboard with sliding panels stretched across one wall. We'd had a grand courthouse built in 1889, but it was taken out by an earthquake in the fifties. The replacement can best be described as utilitarian.

"Mr. Slater?" Judge Love moved her reading glasses down on her nose.

"Your Honor, we have no objection to his testimony as long as he doesn't use the opportunity for anything else."

I hadn't thought of using the opportunity for anything else. Until he mentioned it. Was there an opportunity I hadn't thought of? I remembered a funny video I'd seen of two brothers on Santa's knee. Santa said, "Remember, kids, do your homework. No shortcuts." One boy thought for a second then asked, "If there was a shortcut, what would it be?"

The judge took off her reading glasses and used them to point to me. "Is that clear, Mr. Goodlove? You get up, say you got the letter, and you get down."

"Yes, Your Honor."

"Okay. Motion granted." She tapped her gavel once. "Next. The motion to suppress the presentation of the photographs. Mr. Goodlove?"

Jen stood. "Your Honor, there's always a balance between the probative value of photographs of the deceased and their ability to prejudice the jury. That Ms. Margaux was killed and her body left in the woods is uncontested. In this case, however, most of the violence done to the victim was a result of the remains being eaten and disturbed by a bear and/or other animals. In addition, the body parts had been decomposing for eight days. Thus we ask that the photographs not be shown to the jurors."

"Mr. Slater?"

"Your Honor," he said, "we will need to demonstrate the lack of defensive wounds on the victim. Photographs will make that clear to the jurors. Mr. Goodlove will be free to explain the reasons for the condition of the body."

Judge Love thought about it for only a few seconds. "I am ruling that overview photographs of the corpse and crime scene shall not be allowed unless blurred. I will rule on closeups of individual body parts as necessary." She rapped the gavel.

Chapter Seventeen

DURING THE TRIAL ITSELF, the jury is king. During jury selection, the judge is king. Or queen. The judge decides whether to allow a jury questionnaire, the time limits for voir dire, what questions are appropriate, and so on. Another difference: During the trial, you generally don't want to ask a question unless you know the answer. During jury selection, the opposite is true. It's a fishing expedition. Juror bias is hidden below the surface, and the goal is to hook a big one so you can release the prejudiced juror back into the wild.

We very much wanted Ms. Lynette Vesta on the jury, but we were careful not to let our enthusiasm show. If Slater picked up on it, he might eliminate her with one of his peremptory challenges.

Despite her first name, Ms. Lynette Let-Me-Speak-to-the-Manager Vesta was a "Karen." That's the internet term for a woman who feels entitled to everything being perfect. A neighbor better not leave his garage door open, or she'll bring it up at the next homeowners' association meeting. We knew this because of a tweet she'd posted. At a local restaurant, she'd found the body of a tiny mosquito on her smoked chicken. The waiter hadn't been impressed with her complaint, but after talking with the manager, she got a free dessert. "SCORE!" she'd tweeted.

Jen asked, "Ms. Vesta, during this trial, you may be called upon to make decisions based on scientific evidence. Would you have a problem with that?"

Our data mining had shown that she had a strong anti-science bias. She was a climate-change and moon-landing denier and an anti-masker.

"Well, science is okay as far as it goes, but the world is very complex, and scientists always try to reduce things to a set of equations." She looked around to see if anyone was with her on that. In her forties, her makeup was perfect, and her pearl earrings matched both her necklace and her teeth.

"Thank you, Ms. Vesta." Jen turned to the judge. "We accept Ms. Vesta." Jen's tone suggested she'd like to try to strike the woman for cause—without using up one of our precious peremptory challenges—but knew that would fail.

Slater frowned at me and cocked his head. We wanted him confused. We knew something that apparently he did not: Vesta was an anti-vaxxer. Nicole had located a post on an obscure message board in which the woman had railed against the money-grubbing vaccine companies. She felt that natural immunity was superior and that the companies were bilking the country out of billions of dollars. So, although she didn't care for scientists like Arthur, our case against Spiker and his fake vaccine would resonate with her. We were careful not to high-five when she was seated.

Overall, however, I'd have to put jury selection in the win column for Slater. We'd used up all our peremptory challenges and could do nothing to strike a woman who seemed to feel that all men were pigs. She had a troublesome marriage, but since there had been no documented abuse, we weren't able to eliminate her for cause.

At the end of the proceedings, Arthur whispered, "It would seem that we are at a disadvantage with this jury, is that not so?"

"You never can tell ahead of time, Arthur. Human beings are complex creatures, and we can only scratch the surface when it comes to understanding their thought processes."

"I seem unable to understand Ms. Lynette Vesta's opinion of science. Do many people feel that way?"

I fluttered my lips. "My theory is that some people who do not do well in school resent those who perform well. To make themselves feel better, they declare that feelings are more important than science."

"But you made no effort to strike Ms. Vesta." Arthur had studied up on legal procedures and knew all the jargon.

I glanced at Slater and whispered to Arthur, "I'll tell you later."

I didn't invite Arthur to our final pretrial meeting. He wasn't handling the stress well, and we needed to make a frank assessment of our chances. Also, Nicole wanted to show us something she felt could be devastating to the case if it got out.

The security camera at a gas station in Orick had picked up a white 2019 Honda Civic traveling south soon after Margaux's estimated time of death. The timing worked perfectly, figuring how long it would take Arthur to hike back to the trailhead after the murder and then drive south. There were two points that worked in our favor, however. First, that car model was extremely common. There were no distinguishing marks visible nor was the license plate discernible. The second point was more important: The car was not picked up traveling north. We knew from Margaux's Google Timeline that she had traveled from Redwood Point to the Lost Man Creek Trail, a trip of less than one hour. The only other way to get to the trail from Redwood Point would be to travel inland to Willow Creek and around, requiring at least three hours. Simple conclusion: Margaux hadn't traveled north in Arthur's car. Further, it suggested the Honda Civic seen traveling south was not Arthur's.

Arthur's phone hadn't been recovered, and his timeline was not retrievable from Google's database, known as Sensorvault, because he had apparently never turned on location tracking. It was a setting that is off by default.

Nicole had her laptop open on the small conference table in my office, and Jen and I stood on either side of her.

"Okay," she said. "It was total overkill, but I assumed a four-hour window for when Margaux's phone traveled north to the trail."

I stretched my back. "But the Google data is much more precise than that. To the minute."

"I said it was overkill. I followed Louella's advice and pretended that I was sure Arthur's car had traveled north through Orick within that window. With me?"

We both nodded.

"The gas station is on the east side of Highway 101. I watched all four hours of the footage first at five times normal then at normal speed. I definitely did not see Arthur's car."

I said, "Right, good. We knew that."

"Yes, we did, and so did Slater. Now check out this footage from right when Google says the phone was going north through Orick." She clicked Play, let it run, clicked Pause, and waited.

"Okay, no Honda Civic, right?" Jen said. "Am I missing something?"

"Maybe a little less drama, sweetheart. Just tell us. What's the point?" I squatted down so I could see the screen better.

Nicole checked her notes, advanced the playback to a certain point, and paused it. "There."

"A big truck." I scratched my head. "So?"

"A big semi with an aerodynamic skirt on the trailer that goes almost down to the road surface."

Jen swore in Chinese.

I said, "What am I missing? Oh, *no!*"

Nicole looked at me. "Right. I went up to Orick and measured the distance between some landmarks visible in the video. From that, I calculated that this truck was traveling thirty-five in a forty-five zone. There's a dotted centerline there. Arthur might have been passing it just as it went by the gas station." She tapped the screen. "I'd bet my inheritance Arthur's car is on the other side of that truck. We just can't see it."

"Huh." I took a deep breath and rubbed my chin. "Okay, nice work. It would have been a disaster if they'd blindsided us with that in front of the jury. It's not definite, but—"

"It gets them out of their hole," Nicole said. "They would like the security cam video to place Arthur at the scene, but if he isn't seen driving north, it argues that the southbound Civic isn't his. But if they figure this out …"

"If need be, we can scoff at the improbability of him passing that truck at just the right moment. You definitely can't see anything under the truck?"

"No," Nicole said, "and I looked. But you believed it right away when I pointed it out. And there's no southbound traffic that would have made it impossible to pass."

"Well, we'll hope he doesn't—"

"Slater won't see it," Jen said. "How many hours did you spend on this, Nicole?"

"At least six hours. Maybe eight."

"I don't think they would be able to devote that much time to it. Plus, I'm not sure Derek is capable of that kind of out-of-the-box thinking."

"Well, hold on." I rubbed the back of my neck. "In a sense, it's kind of obvious."

Nicole pointed to her laptop screen. "Sure, once you see it."

"We'll have to be careful not to say anything that would clue Slater in."

"You mean while we're pretending to be righteously indignant that they would even consider presenting that evidence because the car is a common model, and it's only seen traveling south."

"When you say it like that, sweetheart, it sounds—"

"No quizzing please, Dad."

"What?"

"You were going to quiz me on why we shouldn't turn our finding over to the police."

She was right, of course. I cocked my head, pointed to my chest, and mouthed, "Who, me?"

"This is the last time I'm going to respond to you treating me as an intern. We don't bring up this idea because first, we would be disbarred for not acting in the best interest of the client, and second, this is just supposition." She tapped her computer. "We don't know that his car is on the other side of that truck."

"What about the elephant?" Jen asked.

I frowned. "In the room?"

"This is more evidence that Arthur did it. It's significant. We've been telling ourselves that the evidence against him is weak. But ..." Jen waved her hand at the truck, still on the screen.

I stood back up, my knees cracking, walked around the table, and sat. "You know what's different about this case?"

Jen and Nicole just looked at me.

"Well, I'll tell you. This is the first time we know the client isn't lying to us. He can't lie about what he can't remember."

"Unless he's lying about having amnesia," Jen said.

"Yeah, good point. Okay, how about the eyewitness, the teenager? Do we call him?"

Soon after Margaux's murder, the county served a "geofence warrant" for the Lost Man Creek area for a few hours before and after her estimated time of death. Google then supplied anonymized data of all the phones in that area, GPS data that's recorded even when there's no cell coverage. Once they'd identified phones in that region, they served another warrant for more information, this time requesting the names of the phones' owners. Amazing that all of that data is recorded and saved even when the phones have no coverage.

Margaux's phone had traveled up the trail and stopped. Another person had been hiking down the trail and had passed her. This turned out to be a gawky teenage boy from Montana. Louella interviewed him—twice—and although he was able to describe Margaux's "super hot," low-cut top and "sprayed on" tights, he had nothing to say about whoever was with her. He'd said he thought there was someone with her, but that's all.

Jen crossed her arms. "She would have towered over Arthur. If he was with her, I'd think the kid would have mentioned that."

"You're underestimating the power of big-league cleavage on adolescent hormones," I said.

"Still. If it were Arthur—or the scary-looking Spiker, for that matter—I think he'd have noticed."

"I've seen her naked," I said. "I'm surprised the kid isn't still out there, wandering around, bumping into trees, drooling."

Nicole tapped her pen against her chin. "Maybe that tells us it was a normal-sized guy. Someone forgettable. Could we put him on the stand to emphasize that?"

"No, too risky. What if he points to Arthur and says, 'Hey. I remember now. That's him.' Besides, his testimony might suggest she wasn't under duress. We'd like to propose that maybe someone was forcing her along the trail."

"Do you think Slater will call him?"

"Probably not. He'll have the same concerns I do."

"I'll prepare a cross, just in case," Nicole said.

We went through our overall strategy again, and Jen went back to her office.

I asked Nicole, "How you doing, sweetheart?"

"Toby?"

I nodded.

She closed her laptop. "Every morning, when I wake up, I have a blessed fifteen seconds before I remember that he's gone."

"I know what you mean. I'm a little worried that when we're done with this trial, when we're less busy, it's going to hit us harder."

She picked up her laptop and stood. "I think you'll be okay, Dad."

"Because?"

"Why do I think that?"

"Yeah."

She shrugged. "I don't know. You've seemed to bounce back a bit. It's just a feeling."

"What about you?"

She fluttered her lips, something she got from me. "I'm good."

"When this trial is over," I said, "let's you and I spend some more time together."

"Deal. But no more quizzing, right?"

"No more quizzing."

Time for opening statements. Most trials follow the format of a well-prepared lecture: Tell them what you're going to tell them, then tell them, then tell them what you told them. The opening statement was the first of those three parts.

Most of the audience seats were taken since the amnesia aspect of the case had received national attention. The crowd was restless because there had been some procedural delays. The full complement of Goodlove and Shek attorneys sat at the defense table: Jen, Nicole, and me. Arthur sat between me and my daughter.

Slater had one assistant at the prosecution table. My frenemy stepped to the lectern, looking dapper, a hint of his coconut-scented cologne flowing over me as he passed. I suspected he wore a girdle under his tailored gray suit.

"Ladies and gentlemen of the jury," he said, "on May ninth, Arthur Toll took Ms. Margaux Marchand to the forest for a picnic. We will show you that he snuck up behind her, threw a rope around her neck, and strangled her to death." Slater demonstrated, miming pulling the overlapped ends of a rope, grimacing, and straining his voice as he spoke the last four words.

"This is a simple case, and the trial will be mercifully quick. We can't know for sure why the defendant wanted to kill Margaux, a beautiful Frenchwoman in the prime of her life. Perhaps they were having an affair that had gone wrong. Perhaps she wanted to break up with him. But that doesn't matter because we have three pieces of hard evidence that will show you, without a doubt, Arthur Toll is the murderer. First, security camera footage that shows Arthur's car driving away from the trail on which Margaux's body was discovered. Second, right after the murder, the defendant fled the county, hoping we'd never find him. Third and most importantly, Arthur Toll's DNA was found on the murder weapon! But what does he say about all this? What is his defense?"

I relaxed in my chair. He hadn't figured out that Arthur's car had also traveled north.

Slater passed his gaze over the jurors before answering his own question. "Arthur Toll says, get this, 'I … don't … remember … anything.' That's right, the defendant has made the outlandish claim that he has total amnesia. Doesn't even remember his own name, he says. It would be laughable if a young woman hadn't been brutally murdered. At the same time, it's brilliant, isn't it? Questioning an alleged murderer is an important way to discover the truth. But in this case, the defendant's ruse has made it impossible for us to even ask him where he was on the day of the murder. Well, we can ask, but we can't get an answer. Brilliant."

"Now." He scoffed. "The defense is going to try to convince you that someone else from Margaux's company, a Dr. Henry Spiker, killed her. Admittedly, Dr. Spiker is a bad man who had some secrets. The defense will say that this other person killed Marchand and then administered a drug to the defendant to give him amnesia. Sounds almost reasonable, right? But not so fast. Again, there are three clear problems with that."

Slater held up one finger. "First, you'll learn that Margaux's body had no defensive wounds. She was a big, strong woman, so how did this bad guy get her miles out into the forest, which is where she was murdered? If she suspected him of wrongdoing, wouldn't she have resisted?"

After pausing, Slater added a second finger. "Next, wouldn't it have been easier to simply kill Dr. Toll instead of injecting him with a drug? If this other guy killed Margaux, why wouldn't he just do the same to Dr. Toll?

"And finally," he raised a third finger, "this Henry Spiker couldn't have killed her because he was somewhere else on the day of the murder. He has an ironclad alibi."

Another pause. "So, ladies and gentlemen, when my learned and extremely skilled opponent, Mr. Goodlove —" Slater gestured to me "—starts blowing smoke, don't let him obscure the straightforward and simple narrative of this crime: The defendant took Ms. Marchand out for a picnic and then, for whatever reason, snuck up behind her and strangled her with a rope."

I watched Slater return to his seat. Nice job. Unfortunately. Short and sweet. I put my hand on Arthur's forearm. He was trembling. He reached into a pocket and pulled a handkerchief from it. Nicole intercepted him before he could mop his brow and whispered something in his ear.

After stepping to the lectern, I paused, building suspense but also calming myself. *Things are fine. We are prepared. We have a good case.*

"Ladies and gentlemen, as I'm sure you've heard on the news, Dr. Henry Spiker of Vanovax Corporation is under investigation for a heinous fraud, which, had he succeeded, might have led to the deaths of thousands of innocent people around the world. Thousands of people! Can you imagine? He conspired to create a pretend vaccine that was worthless but which would have earned him millions of dollars in ill-gotten gains because of his stock options. What you will learn is that my client, Dr. Arthur Toll, along with his colleague Ms. Margaux Marchand, were onto him. They were looking into this terrible scam. Arthur Toll was unsure of his conclusions, however, and being a religious man of principle, he worried about falsely accusing anyone. At the same time, he was concerned about his safety and the safety of Ms. Marchand, so Arthur gave me a letter to be opened only if something happened to him. You'll see that very letter soon." I find it helps to give the jurors something to look forward to.

"That letter shows that Arthur was in fear for his life and Ms. Marchand's. You'll find out why he didn't go to the police. You'll also learn what a devout Christian Arthur was. Only nine days after I received the letter, Margaux was murdered. At the same time, someone gave Arthur a massive dose of what the media has been calling 'the amnesia drug.' We'll show that this drug has caused irreversible damage to parts of his brain and you'll see that his amnesia is genuine." I didn't mention that Arthur was the lead researcher on propolofan. I'd bring that up later. I wanted to keep things simple for the opening statement.

"The prosecutor says Arthur's DNA was found on the rope, but there's a perfectly innocent reason for that. The prosecutor says Dr. Spiker had an alibi, but we'll show you that the alibi is sketchy. Not reliable. There's no objective evidence that he wasn't at the murder scene. But even if Dr. Spiker didn't personally kill Ms. Marchand, he might have used part of his considerable wealth to have someone else do it. Or perhaps one of his coconspirators killed her to keep her quiet. These were scoundrels who were facing long prison sentences if their secret got out."

I paused again. "To summarize, we'll show you that Dr. Henry Spiker, someone willing to cause the deaths of thousands of innocent people to line his own pockets, murdered Ms. Marchand and attempted to silence Arthur Toll to prevent these brave whistleblowers from exposing his terrible fraud."

Nicole gave me a thumbs up when I returned to the defense table, but I saw something that I hoped the jurors missed: Arthur was slumped in his chair with his chin lowered to his chest. The look of a defeated man.

Chapter Eighteen

SLATER ANNOUNCED, "THE STATE calls Detective Kosmo Lombardi."

We were in Humboldt's largest courtroom, Courtroom 4. The gallery was packed, and spectators stood along the back wall. Some woman was wearing too much perfume. I twisted around and looked but found no obvious candidates.

Lombardi came up the aisle, wearing a heavy herringbone suit jacket, a white shirt, and a maroon checkerboard tie. He was militantly unconventional, and I suspected he'd have been fired if he weren't so good at solving crimes. People used to joke that a mullet is business in the front, party in the back. Lombardi's brown hair was business on the sides with the party on top. It added a few inches to his already tall frame.

After going through the preliminaries, Slater said, "Please tell us … what you saw when you arrived at the scene."

"It was pretty grisly. The body was lying in a small clearing. About sixty yards from the trail. This was May seventeenth. Based on her phone records, Ms. Marchand died on May ninth. So it had been out there for eight days. You can guess the animals ate her up pretty good. We think it was mostly black bears, so the parts were scattered around a lot. Really gruesome."

Slater introduced People's Exhibit 1. "Is this an accurate photo of the scene?"

There were gasps when it came up on the wall displays.

Lombardi adjusted the microphone. He had a funny, jerky way of moving. "Yes, excepting it's been blurred."

"You said she was killed on May ninth. How did you reach that conclusion?"

The detective explained about how the Google Timeline data was obtained then said, "So, her phone traveled to the place we found the body. It moved around a little bit once there then stopped."

"And what time was that?"

"One fourteen in the afternoon."

"That's when she was killed."

I stood. "Objection. Assumes facts not in evidence."

Judge Love scowled at Slater. "Sustained. Mr. Slater, you know better than that." She told the jurors to ignore the question.

Slater gave me a give-me-a-break look. He turned back to Lombardi. "That's when she died?"

Lombardi shrugged. "Near enough. She could have taken a nap first, but she never moved after one fourteen."

"Did she move around much just before she stopped moving?"

"I don't understand."

He understood completely. They'd worked out this exchange, which allowed them to emphasize their point.

Slater asked, "Did she ... run around as if someone were chasing her?"

"Oh, I see. No."

"Did that suggest anything to you?"

"Well, it suggests that she was drugged before she was strangled."

Slater squinted. "How would that work?"

"Someone could have put a drug in her wine. We found a wine bottle nearby."

"No further questions."

I stood and walked to the lectern. "Detective Lombardi, where did you find Ms. Marchand's phone?"

"It was in the side pocket of a little backpack. A bear, presumably, had torn the backpack apart. There had been food in it. We found wrappers and stuff."

"I see. So the phone was in the backpack."

"Objection. Asked and answered." Slater sounded bored.

"Sustained."

"Detective, if you go for a picnic with food in a backpack, what do you do when you get to the picnic site?"

"I stop?"

"And do you put the backpack down?"

"I see. Yeah, maybe."

"There would be no reason to leave it on your back, right?"

"No."

"So, if you're sitting there, having a picnic, possibly with a friend or colleague, and a—" I looked at my notes "—threatening stranger came up to you, you wouldn't pick up the backpack, would you?"

"No."

"Let's say you go on a picnic with a friend or colleague, and someone follows you up the trail then attacks the two of you. Do you pick up the backpack before running away?"

"Objection. Argumentative. Asked and answered."

The judge squinted. "Uh … no. Overruled. But I think you've made your point, Mr. Goodlove. Please move on. You can answer the question, Detective."

"No."

"To be clear, then, the fact that the phone did not move in no way suggests that Ms. Marchand was drugged."

"Yes, I guess so."

"You guess so?"

"That's possible."

"Your Honor, please instruct the witness to answer yes or no."

She turned to him. "That is a yes or no question, Detective Lombardi."

"Yes."

"How long have you been a detective?"

"Thirty years altogether. Twenty in San Francisco and ten here."

"Wow. That's a long time," I said. "During that period, have you ever encountered a victim who was first drugged and then strangled?"

He thought for a while. "I don't recall any, but I'm sure something like that has happened."

"Here's something that bothers me. If you want to kill someone, why drug them first and then strangle them? Wouldn't it just be simpler to administer a lethal dose of drugs?"

"Drugs are complicated."

"Would an MD-PhD with a degree in neuropsychopharmacology, such as Dr. Toll, have any trouble coming up with something that could be added to Ms. Marchand's wine and cause her to die?" I was on thin ice. It was a calculated risk to point out Arthur's drug expertise, but we'd decided that the why-not-just-a-lethal-dose argument was worth it.

"Objection. Calls for speculation. Detective Lombardi isn't an expert in neuropsycho … whatever."

"Your Honor, Detective Lombardi certainly knows about lethal drugs. I'm simply asking him if someone with an MD and a PhD in that field would also have the knowledge necessary to kill someone with a drug."

"Overruled."

"Okay, yes," Lombardi said. "He probably could have poisoned her."

"So there would be no reason to drug her first and then strangle her, is that right?"

"Maybe he didn't want her to struggle."

"In which case, he could have just administered a lethal dose."

"Objection. Argumentative. Mr. Goodlove is badgering the witness."

"Sustained. Please move on."

"Detective Lombardi," I said, "have you uncovered a motive for Arthur to kill Ms. Marchand?"

"Nothing tangible."

"Tangible?"

"No, we don't have a motive."

"You didn't find that Arthur was her lover?"

"No."

"In fact, there was no evidence they were in any kind of relationship outside of their work, is that correct?"

"Correct."

"So Arthur was unlikely to be jealous of another man, is that so?"

"Correct."

"You didn't find that Margaux was about to reveal anything about Arthur—she wasn't blackmailing him?"

"No."

"Were there any other men who had those motives, jealousy or silencing her?"

"Yes, but—"

"Did you investigate any animal rights activists who objected to Ms. Marchand's experimentation on lab animals?"

"No."

"No further questions."

The Humboldt County medical examiner had a strange double chin. Instead of being fat all the way across his neck, it existed only below his chin, like a bulbous turkey wattle. It flopped around when he talked or turned his head. Distracting.

Slater began his questioning. "Dr. Becker, please tell us what you learned from examining the body of Ms. Marchand."

"Right. Unfortunately, Ms. Marchand's body had been out in the woods for eight days, during which time it was depredated by animals. Bears and vultures and perhaps raccoons. As a result, the body parts were spread out over a wide area and in poor condition. Some of them were not recovered."

Arthur's head fell forward, his chin on his chest. Nicole whispered in his ear, and he raised his head up and looked straight ahead. It was rough stuff to hear, but who knew how the jury would interpret his body language? Remorse? They would soon be told that Arthur had no memory of Margaux, so we didn't want them to think he was sad over the loss of his friend.

"Were you able to determine the cause of death?"

"Asphyxiation caused by ligature strangulation."

"Can you put that in layman's terms?"

"Yes. Ms. Marchand was strangled to death with a rope."

"You told us that much of the body was missing," Slater asked, "so how could you tell she was strangled?"

"Well, two things. First, we had enough of the neck to observe abrasions from the rope. These are admittedly light scars, indicating only moderate pressure, but the pressure was enough to compress the carotid arteries and/or jugular veins and cause cerebral ischemia. In addition, there was compression of the laryngopharynx and other structures that would have caused asphyxia. Second, asphyxia was indicated by the petechial hemorrhages above the ligature marks and elsewhere."

They took some time to explain those things in layman's terms and also displayed exhibits related to the injuries.

"Dr. Becker, did you note any defensive wounds on Ms. Marchand's body?"

"I did not."

"What would those have looked like?"

"Usually bruising on the fists or forearms, most often on the dominant arm."

"Did you see any other injuries or bruising that would indicate that Ms. Marchand was fighting for her life?"

Becker scratched his ear. "Nothing recent."

"Was Ms. Marchand's body moved to where she was found?"

"No. That is where she died."

Slater acted puzzled. "But the body was in pieces. How can you tell that?"

Becker explained, going into a little too much detail about how the blood had settled in the body tissues, etc. They moved on.

"Dr. Becker, was Ms. Marchand pregnant?"

"She was."

"How far along?"

"Eleven weeks."

"Do we know who the father was?"

Becker shook his head. "We do not. The defendant is not the father, nor is any man at Vanovax that we tested. We also performed DNA testing on other men who knew the victim, and none were the father. Nor was Ms. Marchand's husband."

Murmurs rippled through the audience and the jurors.

"No further questions."

Jen stood and went to the lectern. She'd put her hair up in a bun, exposing the delicate lines of her neck. I still had trouble believing she'd married me.

"Dr. Becker, have you ever heard the expression, 'The absence of evidence is not evidence of absence'?"

"Yes."

"Can you explain what that means?"

"It means that if you … uh … can't show that something exists, it doesn't mean that it doesn't. Exist. It may mean that you just can't find it. It may be there."

"Thank you." She glanced toward the jury. "Now, you said that many of the body parts were missing. Might that mean there were defensive wounds, but you couldn't see them?"

"Yes."

"You just didn't see them on the parts you examined."

"Correct."

"Was Ms. Marchand right-handed?"

"Yes," he said. "Her right humerus was wider, indicating she was right-handed."

"I see," Jen said. "The humerus is a bone?"

"Yes. The upper arm bone. Here." He held out his arm and pointed to it.

"So the right arm was the dominant arm, and you said that defensive wounds most often appear on the forearm of the dominant arm, is that right?"

"Yeah."

"I'm sorry," Jen said, "can you speak up?"

"Yes, I said that."

"But your examination of the forearm showed the absence of defensive wounds?"

"Well, we couldn't examine that because we never found the right forearm. An animal must have made off with it."

"Absence of evidence."

"Objection," Slater said, rising to his feet. "Ms. Shek is not testifying here."

"Sustained," Judge Love said. "Let me hear a question, Ms. Shek."

"Is it true, Dr. Becker, that your failure to see defensive wounds may simply be due to missing or damaged body parts?"

"Well, there were some places you might expect defensive wounds but which did not have them."

Jen looked up at the judge.

Judge Love told the witness to answer the question.

Becker squirmed in his seat. "Could you repeat the question?"

"Is it true, Dr. Becker, that your failure to see defensive wounds may simply be due to missing or damaged body parts?"

I love it when a witness gives us the chance to emphasize our most important question.

"Yes."

"Have you ever examined the body of a woman attacked by someone she knew?"

"Yes, of course."

"How about a wife killed by a husband?"

"Same answer."

Judge Love said, "Please answer yes or no."

"Yes."

"Did these victims have defensive wounds?"

"Yes, usually."

Jen sighed as if disgusted. "Would this sum up your testimony so far? You failed to find defensive wounds but admit they might be there, and in any case, the lack of defensive wounds doesn't mean the assailant was known to the victim."

"The lack of defensive wounds could mean she was drugged first."

"Hold on, I'm confused. You just admitted that you couldn't conclude there were no defensive wounds. Now you are basing something on the lack of defensive wounds?"

"Objection. Argumentative."

"Overruled, but please reword the question, Ms. Shek."

C'mon, Jen, try to make it less confusing. Cut the double negative.

"Ms. Marchand may have had defensive wounds, is that correct?"

Good!

"Uh, yes."

"And so you can't conclude that she was drugged before being strangled, is that right?"

"Yes."

Without pausing, Jen asked, "Did you find any evidence that drugs had been administered to Ms. Marchand?"

Becker laughed, a little too loudly. "After eight days in the woods? No. Any drugs—"

"Thank you. Did you find any evidence of old wounds on Ms. Marchand?"

"Yes."

"What were those?"

"Both of her clavicles had been broken at some point. She'd had a wrist fracture, an ankle fracture, and two broken ribs."

"Wow. How recent were those?"

"At least a year old. Some older than that."

"Might she have been beaten by someone? A lover?"

"No idea."

"Might she have been involved with some rough characters or an abusive boyfriend who beat her?"

"Not necessarily."

Jen asked. "Are her old wounds typical of someone who has been beaten by a partner?"

"Some of them are, yes."

"Does physical domestic abuse sometimes lead to murder?"

"Sometimes, yes."

"No further questions."

Slater raised his arm, one finger extended. "Redirect?"

"Go ahead."

At the lectern, he asked, "If drugs had been administered to Ms. Marchand, would they have been detectable in the corpse after it had been in the forest for eight days?"

"No, they would not."

"Ms. Marchand's earlier injuries, could they have been caused by participating in rough sports—mountain biking, rock climbing, or skiing, for instance?"

This was my guess, given Margaux's lack of fear when surfing. Her past was a mystery, though. We'd uncovered very little information about her.

"Yes, absolutely," Dr. Becker said.

Slater sat. Jen stood and asked for and was granted permission for recross.

"Dr. Becker, you said that Ms. Marchand might have received these injuries during extreme sports. Do you have any evidence that she was an athlete?"

"Absolutely. Despite the state of the body, we could tell that she had extraordinarily well-developed muscles."

I looked over at Slater. He was frowning, probably wondering why Jen seemed to be knocking down our own homicidal boyfriend theory.

Jen shrugged. "Would it surprise you to hear that she was, in fact, an athlete who had competed in, say, wrestling?"

"Objection. Assumes facts not in evidence."

"Your Honor, I'm simply getting to the nature of her muscular development."

"Overruled, but you are close to crossing the line, Ms. Shek."

Becker said, "Yes, she may have been an athlete of that type."

"She was very strong."

"I expect so, yes."

"How tall was Ms. Marchand?"

"She was quite tall. We estimated her height at six foot three."

"And her weight?"

"Well, that estimate wasn't as easy, but we estimated two hundred pounds, and that fits with the medical records we received."

"So, she was big, very big for a woman, and she was strong."

"Objection. Asked and answered. Compound question."

"Sustained."

Jen looked at me, and I nodded. We'd planned to get to this later, but we decided to strike while the iron was burning hot.

Jen turned to the judge. "I would like to ask Dr. Toll to stand."

"I'll allow it."

"Please stand up, Arthur."

He did so, and I stood, too.

A murmur went through the audience. We'd had a suit tailored for him that emphasized his slight build. He wore shoes with thin soles. I, on the other hand, wore a bulky suit, and the soles of my shoes added an inch to my height. Any more than that, and I wouldn't have respected myself.

"Dr. Becker, Arthur Toll is only five feet five inches tall." She gestured toward us. "My husband and partner, Mr. Goodlove, is six two, meaning that Ms. Marchand was one inch taller than he is. My husband weighs one ninety. She weighed two hundred pounds! Do you think it would be possible for Arthur to strangle this tall Amazon of a woman, even with a rope?"

We'd considered having Arthur act out trying to strangle me, but that could have failed on several levels.

"Maybe," Becker answered.

"Maybe?"

"It might be difficult, but it's entirely possible, especially if she was drugged."

"That again! There's no evidence that she was drugged. Is that correct?"

"Well—"

"Yes or no." Jen was paging through her notes and didn't even look up.

"Yes. Correct."

"Have you ever investigated a case in which someone was drugged and then strangled?"

"No."

"No further questions."

Slater stood. "Redirect, Your Honor?" The term re-redirect would be appropriate, but it isn't used.

Love looked at him. "Seriously?"

"Approach?"

Jen and I joined Slater up at the bench.

"Your Honor," he said, "I only have one brief point to make. Dr. Toll is stronger than he looks."

The judge asked, "Are you going to arm wrestle him?"

Good one! Jen and I smiled.

Slater didn't laugh. "It won't take long."

Judge Love looked at her watch. "Okay, make it snappy. I want to quit for the day."

Back in our places, Slater introduced a new exhibit, one of Arthur's lab notebooks. After a bit of a fuss about establishing the foundation for the notebook, we proceeded. Love was fading fast.

Slater said, "Dr. Becker, this is one of many lab notebooks that Dr. Toll kept. He apparently used it as a daily journal or diary, as well as for his professional note-taking. Can you read the section starting where I placed the Post-it note?"

"Yes. Uh ... 'December nineteen, 2020. After my full year of strength training, I have been gratified with an increase in strength of over thirty percent, yet I have been disappointed at the lack of visible muscle hypertrophy.'" Becker looked up.

"Thank you." Slater sat.

The testimony as a whole wasn't perfect, but the jurors got a feeling for how hard it would have been for Arthur to strangle Margaux. If they could have seen her in action, muscling her way through the surf, they'd have been even more convinced that Arthur wouldn't have stood a chance in a fight with her. Personally, I couldn't see any circumstance under which he could have strangled her.

Slater's attempt to repair the damage done by our physical demonstration was unconvincing. Seeing is believing.

The next day started with testimony about the Honda Civic seen driving south from the crime scene. I was surprised they'd included it; the argument that it was Arthur's car was weak. Part of me worried whether Slater knew, unconsciously, that he had missed something. I wanted to get the damn thing over with because if Slater figured out Nicole's revelation, he'd be much closer to putting Arthur at the scene. Maybe enough to sink us.

The evidence technician displayed the satellite images that showed the jury where the security camera was. He showed the footage of the car driving south, and Slater made the point that the time worked perfectly. It fit the facts if Arthur killed Margaux, hiked back to his car, then drove south.

Nicole took the cross. "Is the Honda Civic one of the most popular cars in Humboldt County?"

"I don't know about Humboldt, but it's a very popular car, yes," the technician answered.

"Could you see the car's license plate?"

"No."

"Could you see the occupant or occupants?"

"No."

"And this car wasn't seen traveling north at any time before the time of death, is that correct?"

I had to make an effort not to glance at Slater.

The tech said, "No."

"Could Arthur have taken a different route from Redwood Point?"

"Well, yes, but it would have been a tedious three-hour drive. It isn't likely."

"Doesn't that imply that the Honda Civic in this video did not, in fact, belong to the defendant but rather belonged to some random tourist driving south along Highway 101?"

"Perhaps."

"Thank you. No further questions."

A drop of sweat trickled from my underarm and down my side. My relief at getting that over with may have been written on my face. I glanced at Slater. He was staring at me with narrowed eyes. *Crap!*

Chapter Nineteen

"THE PEOPLE CALL MS. Odessa Orlano."

She was Dr. Henry Spiker's alibi, swearing she had been with him all day on the ninth of May. We'd interviewed her several times, and there was something off, but I couldn't put my finger on it.

I watched her walk up the aisle. She wasn't alluring physically, with an overly wide nose and a smile sabotaged by misaligned teeth, but her voice! It was a seductive bedroom voice, smooth rather than husky. Maybe it just seemed that way to me because the timbre and Mexican accent made her sound exactly like my first wife, Raquel.

Slater led her through her testimony like the pro he was, endearing her to the jury and engaging in some light banter. He was enjoying his preemptive attack on our contention that Spiker had killed Margaux.

Rather than allowing Orlano's voice to depress me, I let it evoke pleasant memories of Raquel. I wanted to close my eyes and listen, but I needed to watch her body language. Jen did the cross. We'd decided that

Nicole or I might have been distracted by Orlano's voice.

The screens on the wall came to life, showing Orlano in an interview room with unadorned cinderblock walls. Jen introduced the clip. "This is a video of your first discussion with the police."

Playback began.

"Ms. Orlano," Detective Lombardi asked, "Dr. Spiker says you were with him on May ninth, but you are saying you did not spend that day in Willits with Dr. Spiker. Is that right?"

"Absolutely not. I met him at a party a few days earlier, but that is all. I was with my husband on May ninth."

Jen paused the playback. "That sounds very convincing, Ms. Orlano. You're telling us you were lying when you said that?"

Orlano dropped her head. "Yes, I was."

"You are a very convincing liar. I'm impressed." Jen waved her hand at the screen, where Orlano's earnest face was frozen.

"Objection. Argumentative." Slater's objection was spot-on. An attorney is not supposed to voice her interpretation of the evidence.

"Sustained."

"Are you a good liar, Ms. Orlano?" Jen asked.

"I wanted to protect my marriage. I love my husband very much."

Jen looked at the judge.

Judge Love turned to the witness. "Please answer the question, Ms. Orlano."

"No." She shrugged. "Maybe."

"Would you say that you lied convincingly in that video?"

Orlano's crooked teeth raked her lower lip. "I said what I had to to protect my—" She glanced over at the judge. "Yes."

"But just one month later, you contacted the police to confess that you had indeed spent the day in Willits with Dr. Spiker. Is that correct?"

"Yes."

"The police didn't contact you; you called them?"

"Yes."

"What about your marriage?"

"My conscience bothered me. I didn't want Henry to face a trial for something I knew he didn't do. He was with me on the day that woman was killed."

"We know that you lied on one of those occasions. You either lied when you said you weren't with him or when you said you were. Which are we to believe?"

"I was together with him on May ninth."

I started to worry that the jury would begin feeling sorry for Ms. Orlano, but Jen wasn't done.

"Ms. Orlano, in California, the penalty for lying to the police is a fine of one thousand dollars and up to six months in prison. However, the penalty for lying in a court of law is imprisonment of up to four years in a state prison. Would you like to reconsider what you are telling us?"

That was the moment my total attention to Orlano's body language paid off. For a split second, her eyes widened, almost bulging out of her face. *Terror.* I looked over at the jurors. *Damn, they didn't notice!* I would have seen some recognition. All I saw was empathy.

After the testimony, Jen, Nicole, and I huddled, leaning over the defense table, our heads almost touching.

I asked Jen, "Did you see her eyes? She was terrified."

She squinted and shook her head.

"I think you were looking at your notes. What about you, Nicole?"

"Maybe."

"Maybe?" I whispered. "It was there. Orlano. Is. Lying." I looked back into the audience. Louella was in the back row, and she had her eye on Odessa's husband.

"But why did she deny it at first?" Jen asked.

I turned back. "I don't know. I don't know. But if we can convince the jury that the alibi is false, we're home free. It'll be even better than if he had no alibi."

Slater's expert witness was likable, but I didn't like her. That was a problem. If the jurors liked her, it wouldn't matter that she didn't have the right scientific background to judge whether Arthur's amnesia was real or fake. Of course, I was biased.

Dr. Monica West was thirty-two but seemed younger. Her blond hair was freakishly long, and when she smiled, her upper gums were too prominent.

At the start of her testimony, Slater ran her through her qualifications. She had a PhD from Stanford and headed a group of psychologists who helped senior citizens with their memory issues. That was all. It told me that he'd had trouble finding an expert who could cast doubt on Arthur's amnesia. Next, he got her to relate a few anecdotes about her work, obviously letting her pleasant personality and gentle voice win over the jury.

I stood. "Objection. Relevance."

"Sustained," Judge Love said. "Let's move on, Mr. Slater."

Slater flipped to a new page on his legal pad. "Dr. West, do you think the defendant's alleged amnesia is real?"

"I have never heard of a case of genuine amnesia as complete as his."

After I objected that the answer was nonresponsive, West said, "I was unable to confirm his amnesia in any objective way."

I stood again. "Objection. Your Honor, it's obvious she doesn't want to answer the question."

The judge picked up her gavel and pointed it at me. "Mr. Goodlove, you crossed the line with that comment. Overruled."

Huh. The objection was valid, so she seemed to be punishing me for trying to interpret the answer for the jury. Not a big enough deal to form the basis for an appeal, but it didn't matter. I'd gotten my point across.

The rest of direct included a lot of psychobabble that didn't quite answer the central question. Dr. West was so good at pivoting that she could have gotten a job as a presidential press secretary.

My turn. "Dr. West, I noticed that you do not have a medical degree."

"My PhD is in clinical and physiological psychology." She flashed her gummy smile.

"Do you have an MD degree?"

"No, I do not."

"At issue today, Dr. West is whether Dr. Toll's brain was physically altered in such a way as to cause a profound amnesia. Do you have any experience in neurology?"

She nodded. "I attended neurology rounds at the Stanford Medical Center for two semesters."

"Neuroanatomy?"

"I took a graduate-level course in general anatomy, which included the anatomy of the brain."

I introduced a new exhibit and displayed it on the screens. "Dr. West, can you tell me if you see any abnormalities in this MRI?"

She looked at it for a while. "I would have to examine it closely."

The MRI wasn't of Arthur's brain. It was completely normal. West knew there were abnormalities reported in his scans, and I'd hoped she would parrot back something from the report, but she didn't bite. Too bad.

"Dr. West, yes or no, do you believe Dr. Arthur Toll is faking his amnesia?"

"I can't answer yes or no. My answer is maybe."

"I see. So there's reasonable doubt as to whether he's faking."

"That's fair. Yes," she said.

"Earlier, you said that you couldn't confirm his amnesia in an objective way. Is that right?"

"Yes. There are no tests for retrograde amnesia. Only for anterograde amnesia."

"So, retrograde refers to losing old memories, while anterograde refers to the inability to remember new things. Is that right?"

"Basically. Research into memory—"

"Thank you." I didn't want to give her the opportunity to show off her knowledge. "Did you perform any tests of anterograde amnesia on Dr. Toll?"

"Yes." She livened up a bit. "I performed the TOMM test, the Test of Memory Malingering."

"What does 'malingering' mean?"

"It refers to pretending or exaggerating an illness in order to achieve a gain, such as not having to work."

"Without going into detail, can you explain that test?"

"It's simple. The patient is evaluated on how well he or she remembers images."

"I'm confused," I said. "How does that tell you whether someone is faking their anterograde amnesia?"

"Malingerers almost always perform at a level below chance. It shows they're consciously trying to get the answers wrong. Pretending not to remember."

"And how did Dr. Toll perform?"

She flashed her gums at me. "Actually, he performed very well. He remembered all fifty images. It was remarkable."

"So, absolutely no faking."

"With regard to anterograde amnesia, no."

"Do you think that if he were faking his retrograde amnesia, he might not want to perform well on any memory task?"

"Objection. He's asking her to speculate on the defendant's state of mind," Slater said.

I looked at him and mouthed, "Seriously?" Turning to the judge, I laughed. "Dr. West is a psychologist. Judging Arthur's state of mind is what Mr. Slater brought her here to—"

"Overruled."

Dr. West said, "Yes. If he were faking retrograde amnesia, you might expect him to fake anterograde amnesia as well."

"In summary, you have performed no tests that led you to doubt Arthur's amnesia is real. Is that correct?"

"I simply cannot believe, based on my experience and analysis of the research, that any person could have such a profound—"

"Objection," I yelled. "Nonresponsive."

"Sustained," the judge said. "Dr. West, please do not give any testimony that is beyond the scope of the question."

I repeated the question, and West confirmed that she wasn't able to disprove Arthur's amnesia.

On redirect, of course, Slater asked for her professional opinion, and she answered, "Based on my years studying memory, my experience with patients, and my analysis of the science, I simply cannot believe that any person could have such a profound amnesia as is being claimed in this case."

I checked out the jurors while West was answering. They seemed to like the answer from the very likable psychologist. Even the anti-science woman was nodding her head, perhaps because West's answer was based on a gut feeling.

Slater saved his best for last. The prosecutor's biggest failing was that he often dragged things out, boring the jurors, but with the county's expert on DNA and materials on the stand, he played it just right. Short and sweet.

Toward the end, he said, "To summarize …" Slater's pause was dramatic. "… you found the DNA of the defendant, and only the defendant, on the murder weapon. The rope. Is that correct?"

Jen stood. "Objection. Asked and answered."

"Sustained. Are you done, Mr. Slater?"

"I am, Your Honor." He sat.

Jen was the point person on this, and she made a valiant attempt to limit the damage. "Dr. Young, could you tell how old the DNA on the rope was?"

"I could not." He had a raspy voice, appropriate for his age.

"So it could have been deposited on the rope a month before the murder, is that right?"

"Yes, that's possible."

Jen nodded. "So if Arthur visited Ms. Marchand, say, in April, and handled the rope, his DNA might have been deposited on the rope then."

"Well, the skin cells from his hand would have been sloughed off only if the rope were pulled on strongly."

"I see. If Arthur had been at Ms. Marchand's and used the rope to pull on something, he might have deposited skin cells at that point?"

"Yes, that is conceivable."

"Approach the witness, Your Honor?"

"You may."

"Dr. Young, this is a transcript from the testimony of Humboldt's medical examiner, Dr. Felix Becker. Could you read the part that I've highlighted?"

He cleared his throat. "'Mr. Slater: You told us that much of the body was missing, so how could you tell she was strangled? Mr. Becker: Well, two things. First, we had enough of the neck to notice abrasions from the rope. These are admittedly light marks, indicating only moderate pressure, but the pressure was enough to compress the carotid arteries and/or jugular veins and cause cerebral ischemia.'"

"Thank you. I'll direct your attention to the words 'only moderate pressure.' Would moderate pressure have been enough to deposit the skin cells?"

Young shook his head. "That's impossible to know."

"But if Arthur had visited Ms. Marchand and used the rope to, say, pull a post out of the ground, he would surely have left DNA behind, is that right?"

"Well, yes, but the rope was short."

"But you testified that the rope had been cut from a longer length found at Ms. Marchand's house."

"Yes, that's true."

"So is your evidence consistent with Arthur's having handled that section of rope at Ms. Marchand's when it was part of a longer piece, and not handling the rope when she was murdered?"

"Yes, except that no one else's DNA was found on the rope."

"Of course not!" Jen said. "Because only light pressure had been applied to the rope when she was strangled."

Slater stood to object, but Jen added, "Is that not reasonable?"

Young sighed. "Yes, that's possible."

"And Ms. Marchand's DNA was not found on the rope, even though it was cut from a length of rope at her house?"

"Yes. If she handled it lightly, there might not have been enough material deposited to show up with our test."

Jen frowned. "Okay, this is a little complicated, so I want to make sure I've got it right. It's possible that Dr. Toll was at Ms. Marchand's house, used the rope to pull on something, depositing skin cells. Then later, the rope was cut, and someone else used it to strangle her, but without squeezing it hard enough to deposit skin cells. Is that reasonable?"

"Objection. Asked and answered."

"Sustained."

Jen sat, and I gave her a discreet thumbs up. She had done as well as possible.

"Mr. Slater, do you have any more witnesses?"

"The prosecution rests."

Thank goodness. I closed my eyes and sighed. I wasn't relieved by any weakness in his case—it was stronger than I would have liked—but because after those three words, Slater could not bring up the possibility that Arthur's car had traveled north but been obscured by a truck. His narrowed-eyes stare after the tech's testimony told me he'd suspected something was up. And once he clamped his bulldog jaws onto a problem, he didn't let go until he'd solved it.

But in this case, he hadn't solved it in time.

Chapter Twenty

I'D NEVER BEEN A witness before. A courtroom looks different from the witness stand. It's like being on the stage as opposed to being in the audience. Even when standing at the lectern, questioning a witness, my back is to the audience.

I wasn't nervous about having so many eyes on me, but I was eager to get our side of the story out. We were starting at the beginning, with the letter Arthur had asked me to read only if something happened to him.

Months earlier—it seemed like a lifetime—Slater hadn't objected to my appearing as a witness *as long as I didn't use the opportunity for anything else.* I'd racked my brain to figure out what he meant and came up with only one possible trick: I could read the letter dramatically, emphasizing the parts that favored our defense.

Nicole stood and stepped to the lectern. I smiled. *What an accomplishment to raise a daughter like her.* I put my hand on my chest. *Is my heart actually swelling with pride?*

"All right," she said, "Mr. Goodlove, can you tell us what happened on April thirtieth of this year?"

"Dad."

"Pardon me?"

"I think you can call me 'Dad,' sweetheart."

That got a good laugh. I've found that something in a sitcom or movie that would barely rate a chuckle can kill in the serious setting of a courtroom.

"On that morning," I continued, "Dr. Arthur Toll brought me a sealed envelope."

"At this time," Nicole said, "I would like to introduce Defense Exhibit One." She went through the mechanics of introducing the letter. "May I approach the witness, Your Honor?"

"You may."

She handed me the material. "Would you please read the letter to the court?"

I cleared my throat dramatically. "'Redwood Point, California, April twenty-eight, 2021. My dear Mr. Goodlove. If you are reading this, I may have been killed or injured in such a way as to render me incommunicado.'" I emphasized the words "or injured." At the end, I stopped and looked up at the jurors to see how they were taking it. Some were literally on the edge of their seats. *This really does feel like being on a stage. In a play.*

I looked back down. "'If such is the case, please allow my suspicions, described herein, to guide an investigation into the vaccine department at Vanovax Corporation. I was hesitant to reveal those suspicions —'" I looked up "'—because I considered them insubstantial.'" I'd hoped to convey how nice a guy

Arthur was that he didn't want to falsely accuse anyone. Not sure if that came through.

I continued reading, emphasizing the part where Arthur had innocently overheard the conversation in which someone said the FDA had their heads up their asses. The jurors learned that Arthur was afraid that the bad actors at Vanovax suspected him of snooping around.

I finished up "'... If anything happens to me, please provide this letter to the police ... P.S., I believe Ms. Margaux Marchand—'" I projected my voice when saying her name and looked up before resuming "'— may also suspect misdeeds in the vaccine department.'" After yet another pause, I said, "Let me repeat that. 'P.S. —'"

"Objection! Your Honor, Mr. Goodlove is dramatizing this as if he's Sir Anthony Fucking Hopkins." No, of course he didn't add the swear word, but knowing Slater, he wanted to. "But this has gone far enough. Nonresponsive."

"Sustained. Are you two done?"

"One more question, Your Honor."

The judge thought for a second then spoke. "Go ahead."

"Mr. Goodlove," Nicole said, "under what circumstances did you open the letter?"

"On May tenth, Detective Sergeant Edith Granville informed me that Arthur Toll was missing. I immediately opened the letter Arthur had given me, and, in the presence of Detective Sergeant Granville, I read it aloud."

"Thank you." Nicole sat.

The judge said, "Mr. Slater?"

"No questions, Your Honor."

The judge allowed us a twenty-minute recess. Maybe she felt I needed some downtime following my Oscar-worthy performance.

After months of discussion, we still hadn't decided whether to call our next witness. We convened in the attorney-client conference room, which smelled of cigarette smoke. *Someone broke the rules.* Nicole, Jen, Arthur, and I sat around the ancient table.

I sighed. "Okay, let's vote. Nicole?"

"Yes."

"Jen?"

"Definitely not."

I said nothing.

"Dad?"

I rubbed a pain in my neck. "I could go either way."

Arthur raised his hand. "Might the judge or the jury conclude that we were complicit in any way with regard to his testimony?"

Arthur had been busy soaking up legal knowledge, and we increasingly took advantage of his off-the-charts intelligence. With his speed-reading ability, he'd been filling his tank with both science and law fuel.

"It's always possible, but I doubt it," I said. "Lee went to the police, not to us. His statement to them should match his testimony today. If we call him."

"In that case, I would expect little downside to putting him on the stand."

Jen leaned back. "Louella interviewed him twice. Once, he seemed fine. The other, batshit crazy."

"So, fifty-fifty chance he'll be okay on the stand." I crossed my arms.

"I should remind you," Arthur said, "that statements of probability speak only to our knowledge of the truth, and not the truth per se. Thus we can't assume we will enjoy even odds of effective testimony."

I frowned, not sure what that meant.

"But as I said before," he continued, "even if his testimony is less than efficacious, the downside is negligible."

"Okay, we'll call him." I slapped the table, and we trooped back to the courtroom.

Once everyone was settled in, Nicole stood. "The defense calls Roscoe Lee Redmayne to the stand."

When nothing happened, we turned. Roscoe was sitting in the back row, writing in some kind of scrapbook.

"Roscoe Redmayne," Nicole called out, louder this time

Still nothing. After some gesturing and pointing, the person next to our witness poked him in the shoulder. He jumped and looked up. His scrapbook fell to the floor. He picked it up, worked his way to the aisle, and headed to the witness box.

Roscoe Lee was nineteen and thin as a stick. He wore a half-baked smile and a hat shaped like a train engineer's cap, but green rather than blue and white.

He was sworn in. "You do solemnly state that the testimony you may give in the cause now pending before this court shall be the truth, the whole truth, and nothing but the truth, so help you God?"

"I do." Even with just those two words, his deep Louisiana accent came through. Like *Ahh diew*.

He settled into the witness chair. Judge Love asked him to remove his hat.

"Oh, sorry, ma'am." He was red haired and full of freckles.

"Thank you for coming in today, Mr. Redmayne," Nicole said.

Roscoe smiled and shrugged.

"Can you tell us what you did on May fifteenth?"

"Yeah. I was still here in Redwood Point because I was fixing my car. Waiting for a part, you know? That's when I saw—"

"Excuse me!"

I looked around, not sure where that had come from, then I saw it. An older juror in the front row had her hand up. The bailiff went to her. She wrote something on a notepad, ripped off the page, and handed it to the bailiff, who took it to the judge. I guessed the woman was hard of hearing, and Roscoe's thick accent made him unintelligible. Sure enough, the bailiff handed her a pair of headphones. She mouthed, "Thank you" to the judge.

Nicole turned back to Roscoe. "What did you see?"

"I saw that story on CNN: *Does the World's Top Amnesia Scientist Have Amnesia?* It had a photo of Dr. Toll here." He nodded toward Arthur. "That gave me a chuckle, but I scrolled on to other articles. I left Starbucks and went to check on the part, but it hadn't come in yet. That's when it hit me. I'd seen that guy, the one in the article. I went back to Starbucks and checked the article, and sure enough, that was the guy I saw."

"And what did you do then?"

"I went right to the police and told them."

"On what date did you see Dr. Toll?" Nicole asked.

"It was on Sunday, May ninth. I remember because that was the day my car died. It happened on a Sunday afternoon, and I couldn't get to the auto parts store before it closed."

Despite his accent, which made me think of him as a hillbilly, he was articulate. Well-spoken.

"Can you tell me exactly where and when you saw Dr. Toll?"

"Sure, yeah. He was in Loleta, which I learned is pronounced like the book by Vladimir Nabokov. I stopped there to see the cheese factory, but it had shut down. I thought it might be open even though it was a Sunday, but I found that it's permanently closed. I wandered around the small town and took some pictures. That's when I saw him on a bench near the old railroad tracks."

That was the first I'd heard of photographs. I was going to signal Nicole, but she caught it, too.

"Do you think Dr. Toll was in any of those pictures?" Her voice had gone up in pitch.

"Nah. I went back and looked, but he wasn't."

"Loleta is fifteen miles south of Redwood Point?"

He laughed. "You'd know better than me. I'm not from around here."

"How sure are you that it was Dr. Toll that you saw?"

"Pretty certain. It was either him or someone who looked just like him."

Wish he hadn't phrased it like that.

"Did the police follow up with you?"

"Nah. Remember this was before that woman's body was found. It was just a missing person, so I don't think they gave it much priority. I don't know, but I do know they didn't contact me again."

"Thank you. No further questions."

Slater stood. "Mr. Redmayne, did you talk with Dr. Toll?"

"No, sir."

"Did you sit next to him on the bench."

"No, I did not."

"About how close did you—"

"Shut up!" Roscoe frowned.

What? Every soul in the courtroom froze. The wall clock ticked off the seconds. Tick. Tick. Tick.

Slater said, "Pardon me?"

Roscoe laughed. An embarrassed laugh. "Sorry. Nothing."

Slater looked down at his notes, turned the page, wrote something.

After thirty seconds, Judge Love said, "Mr. Slater?"

"Just a second please, Your Honor."

I watched his gears turning, and then he made the leap that was sure to sink our witness. And our case.

"Mr. Redmayne," he said, "do you hear voices?"

The kid gave his nervous laugh again. "Sometimes. I'm okay, though."

"Are you schizophrenic?"

"Something like that, yeah. I'm okay, though."

Slater narrowed his eyes. "Did the voices tell you that you'd seen Dr. Toll?"

"No, they didn't. Not at all."

"Did they tell you to go to the police?"

"No! No, the opposite."

"Opposite?"

"They told me that it wasn't Dr. Toll. They told me *not* to go to the police."

Slater let that hang in the air for a few moments then said, "Thank you. No further questions."

I had a picture in my head of Slater asking if he could talk to the voices, like a seance or something.

Nicole popped up. "Roscoe, despite the voices, do you think you saw Dr. Toll in Loleta on May ninth?"

"Yes. That's what I think."

"No further questions."

Chapter Twenty-One

OUT IN THE HALL, Slater grabbed my arm. "Conference room. Now."

I pulled it away. "I'm confused. Do I work for you?"

"Sorry." He didn't sound sorry. "Garrett, can we talk, please?"

I followed him into the now-less-smoky conference room and closed the door. "If this is about that kid—"

"It's not." He laughed. "That couldn't have been better if I'd planned it. His voices told him it wasn't the defendant. Oh, man! I'll be telling that story for years." He laughed some more.

"Then what?"

"The truck."

"What truck?"

"The one that was hiding Toll's car when he drove north to murder Ms. Marchand. You need to practice your poker face, buddy. I knew something was up when Nicole was grilling our tech. It took me a while to put the pieces together, but I did. That truck passed the gas station exactly when Marchand's phone said she was in Orick. Toll was on the other side of it."

I shook my head. "Bummer that you've rested your case, huh?"

"Twenty years. Your boy could be out in ten." Slater's offer of a plea deal.

"I'll present it to him, but he won't go for it."

Slater held his arms out, palms up. "He's guilty, and he doesn't even know it, for God's sake."

"I thought you didn't believe in the amnesia."

"Does he know about the truck thing?"

I nodded.

"I'll bet that even *he* thinks he did it."

"Well, *I* know he didn't do it," I said.

"What, you looked deep into his eyes or something?"

"We're done here, Derek."

Slater stepped into my personal space. "You know what's a bummer for *you*?" He tapped my chest with his index finger.

"What's that?"

"You have to win this one. If there's a mistrial, we'll retry him, and telling the jury about the truck hiding his car, it will be a lead-pipe cinch."

On the way out, I said, "Not worried."

I *was* worried, but I hoped the tsunami of reasonable doubt we were about to unleash on the jury might turn the tide. So to speak.

Louella hung up the phone and slid her sleeping cat off the laptop keyboard. Lisbeth was seven months old, still a kitten, and didn't wake up. *Wish I could sleep like that.*

Odessa Orlano, the woman who'd provided the dubious alibi for Henry Spiker, was out of town, but Louella had found the address of the Airbnb where she was staying.

Louella's phone rang. Inspector Granville's face was on the display.

"Edith. What've you got?"

"I've got Arthur Toll's car."

Louella sat back in her chair. "Well, blow me down."

"Indeed."

"Where did you find it?"

"At the bottom of the Eel River, near Ferndale."

Louella took a puff on her vape pen. "Deep enough to hide a car?"

"Barely. A kayaker found it. It's at the motor pool garage at second and J. I assume you'd like to go over it?"

Louella consulted her calendar app. "I'll do it this afternoon."

Nicole had come up with the brilliant idea of using another propolofan researcher as our amnesia expert. Dr. Keisha Zaidel worked for Arthur's competition, an NIH-funded lab in New Jersey. Dr. Zaidel was thirty-five but looked to be in her twenties. That impression was fueled by her complexion—the smoothest and blackest that I'd ever seen.

On her way to the witness stand, she leaned over the defense table and took Arthur's hand. "Arthur, I'm very sorry this happened to you. Know that you and I were friends, and you were an amazing scientist."

Arthur looked at her with no recognition in his eyes. "Thank you."

After she was sworn in, Nicole ran her through her qualifications. Like Arthur, she was an MD-PhD, with degrees from Yale, UCLA, and Cornell. Her PhD was in neuroanatomy as opposed to Arthur's in neuropsychopharmacology.

"Dr. Zaidel, please tell me about your research."

"Certainly. My group at Cornell is researching the amnesic effects of propolofan, the same drug that Arthur's lab was studying."

"You were in competition with Vanovax, is that correct?"

"Yes, in a sense. We both wanted to be the first to prove the drug's potential to help severely depressed patients. I say 'in a sense' because, thanks in part to Arthur, it was a friendly competition. We sometimes shared data. May I say something about Arthur?"

Nicole nodded. "Please."

"Anyone who knew Arthur would realize that he could never commit murder. I got to know him at scientific conferences, and not only is he deeply religious, something that's somewhat unusual for scientists, but there's one other characteristic that he has. It may sound derogatory, but it's not. Here it is. Arthur is meek. He didn't have a lot of friends because he was so devoted to his work, but ask any one of them, and they'll agree that he was kind. I'm sure he still is."

"Do you think his amnesia is genuine?"

"Absolutely, and I can demonstrate it objectively. Can we see the slides I prepared?"

Nicole introduced the exhibits, and the first image was displayed on the screens.

"Please interrupt me if I get too technical. This slide shows an MRI—a magnetic resonance image—from a normal brain on the left and from Arthur's brain on the right. It shows an area of necrotic—sorry, dead—tissue right here." She circled it with a laser pointer. "It's not present in the normal brain. Here. Note the difference in the shade of gray." She used the laser pointer again. "This is a region known as the temporal pole of the prefrontal cortex. I know that's a mouthful, but all you have to understand is that this is an area concerned with episodic memory."

"Episodic?"

"Sorry, memories of things that happened to you." Dr. Zaidel smiled.

I made a note to use her if I ever needed an expert witness concerning the brain.

"But how could it be that Arthur doesn't remember anything from his past, yet he's able to speak three languages, read, write, and so on? Isn't that impossible?"

"Not at all." Zaidel swept her hand across the room. "Everyone here has experienced amnesia just like Arthur's."

Nicole's jaw dropped, but of course it was an act. They'd gone through the testimony ahead of time. "What do you mean? I know I haven't experienced amnesia."

"Do you remember learning how to walk?"

"No, but that was when I was a baby. How could I remember that?"

"What's your earliest memory?"

Nicole pretended to think for a while. "I remember that on my third birthday my dad said, 'You're a big girl now.'"

"That sounds about right. The phenomenon is called 'childhood amnesia.' Most people are unable to retrieve episodic memories from before the age of three, but it can vary from two to eight. The point here is that none of us remember things we experienced before that age, but we retain the skills we learned—walking, speaking, potty training. You remember how to speak, but you don't remember actually learning to speak. Same with walking. Although the neurological mechanisms are different in Arthur's case, the basic idea is the same. Arthur can't remember things he did, but he retains things he learned. It's very real."

"Thank you for that fascinating testimony, Doctor."

Slater made the wise decision. "No questions."

Next, we called the forensic psychiatrist we'd hired to evaluate Arthur. The middle-aged Dr. Tobias Gruber looked serious and intelligent, with wire-framed glasses and a salt-and-pepper beard. He wore a blue sweater over a blue-checked Oxford shirt, tan corduroy pants, and penny loafers.

After running through his impressive qualifications and emphasizing that he was a PhD as well as an MD, Nicole asked, "Dr. Gruber, do you believe Arthur Toll's amnesia is genuine?"

"I do."

"But we've heard testimony that there is no objective test for retrograde amnesia. How did you come to that conclusion?"

"In two ways. I spent over five hours talking with him and evaluating him. Nothing from those conversations suggested that he was dissembling. Lying."

Nicole put her fingertips against her chin and cocked her head. "Could he have simply been a good liar?"

"It's unlikely, but to be sure, I used a second way of evaluating him. Something that's completely objective." He looked at the jury. "First, I'll have to explain something about human physiology. Our bodies often react to stimuli in autonomic ways that are not under the control of our conscious minds."

Dr. Gruber leaned forward to the microphone and looked left and right as if he were about to whisper some secret. He waited for the suspense to build. "*Boo!*" he yelled. The PA system went into feedback, adding more volume to his exclamation.

Every person in the courtroom jumped. Even Nicole, who knew what to expect.

When the laughing died down, Dr. Gruber explained, "None of you in this room made a conscious decision to jump. Your startle responses were not under your control. In the same way, but more subtly, your unconscious mind reacts differently to a face it recognizes than to a face it does not recognize.

"I showed Dr. Toll images of celebrities from the past and also pictures of random people he'd never seen. I saw that his body's response was the same when shown famous versus unknown faces. By measuring his body's autonomic responses to the photos, such as pupil diameter, respiration rate, and—"

Slater popped up. "Objection. Approach, Your Honor?"

We'd anticipated the objection, of course. That's why we had Dr. Gruber describe the results before revealing his method.

Nicole, Slater, and I went up to the bench.

Slater said, "Your Honor, what Dr. Gruber is describing is a polygraph exam. Lie detector evidence is not admissible unless both parties agree to it, and I don't remember agreeing to anything like that."

"Not at all, Your Honor." Nicole used her most confident voice. "This was not a polygraph exam. Dr. Gruber simply used his instruments to get an objective measure of Arthur's recognition response. Gruber never asked, 'Do you recognize this person?' In that case, it would have been a lie detector test. This was not."

Judge Love looked at the far wall and rolled her shoulders. She had on a white scarf that day. Up close, the paleness of her complexion was obvious. "What measurements were taken?"

Nicole checked her notes. "Heart rate, blood pressure, respiration, and skin conductivity."

Slater threw his arms up. "Behold! It looks like a duck, walks like a duck, and quacks—"

"Shush." Love glared at him.

Slater lowered his voice. "Judge, the rules about polygraph evidence are in place because it hasn't been proven to be reliable."

"Not reliable for detecting lies," Nicole said, "but in this case, it's being used for something completely different. It's as though the test measured how much a person jumped when someone yelled, 'Boo.'"

"Can you cite any cases, Ms. Goodlove?" the judge asked.

"There are none. This situation is unique, as you can imagine."

"Let me think a minute." Judge Love looked at nothing, breathing deeply. After a full two minutes, she said, "Polygraphs are suspect because it hasn't been shown that the respondent can't fake the results. Because the same might be true of this so-called recognition response, I'm not going to allow testimony about the test."

When we'd all returned to our tables, the judge addressed the jury. "You are to ignore all testimony from the witness pertaining to any objective measures of Dr. Toll's alleged amnesia." She turned to Nicole. "Any more questions, counselor?"

"No, Your Honor."

"Mr. Slater?"

"No questions, Your Honor."

Even Nicole wasn't too disappointed. Sure, it would have been nice to show the jury that the wiggly lines looked the same when Arthur had been shown a photo of Albert Einstein versus some random messy-haired guy, but we got our point across. The "boo" demonstration, despite the judge's instructions, was not something they could forget or ignore.

Of course, the amnesia was sort of a side issue because his guilt or innocence didn't depend on it, but we wanted jurors to see Arthur as a good guy, not a scammer.

* * *

Arthur's 2019 Honda Civic stood off by itself in Humboldt County's motor pool garage. The car was intact but covered in a layer of light brown mud and green algae. It smelled like low tide. Louella walked around it. *Did Arthur really try to hide it?*

Louella bantered a bit with the garage manager, someone she hadn't seen in ten years, then she put on her evidence collection suit, gloves, and booties and went to work. She psyched herself up by pretending she knew there was something important in there, and she just needed to find it. Garrett had told her that a second interview with Ms. Orlano was the top priority, but he also still hung on to the idea that the lab journal might hold important evidence of Arthur's innocence. They'd included it in their list of exhibits during discovery so if she found it, they could use it. But the trial would wrap up in less than a week. Time was short, and Louella wasn't optimistic.

Humboldt's top fingerprint technician had failed to raise any prints. Prints can survive submersion but only for a few weeks. Arthur's car had been in the slow-flowing Eel River—near the historic Fernbridge— for five months.

It didn't take long to learn that the lab notebook was not in the car, and after two hours of searching, she'd turned up nothing of value. At lunchtime, she sat outside on a bench and unwrapped her pastrami and cheese on rye. She washed the sandwich down with a Michelob Ultra.

Louella was two hours into her next session when she stopped. She retrieved her flashlight and magnifying glass and looked into the space between the driver's seat cushion and the plastic seat control panel. A small piece of paper was stuck there. She phoned the evidence technician, and together they dried the small piece of paper in place then pulled it out.

It was a receipt. Louella was surprised it was readable, but the technician told her that receipts often survived long periods of submersion. It helped that the paper had been protected from the mud by being squeezed between the seat and the plastic. The receipt was for a purchase from the AutoZone parts store in Fortuna on Tuesday, May 11, at 8:12 a.m. Two days after Margaux was killed.

Chapter Twenty-Two

THE ONLY MOTIVE FOR the murder Slater had offered up was that Arthur and Margaux might have had a romantic relationship that went south. We countered by presenting two witnesses from Vanovax who testified they'd seen no evidence of that. Both mentioned Arthur's high ethical standards. Slater brought up the surfing outing, but one of the witnesses explained that Margaux had simply heard of the invitation and was eager to learn surfing herself.

Next, we started on the presentation of our alternate theory of Margaux's death: Dr. Henry Spiker killed her and injected Arthur so no one would discover his vaccine scam. Did I believe this was what happened? Maybe, although I couldn't see Spiker injecting Arthur instead of just killing him. Too complicated and risky.

The Arthur I'd come to know couldn't—either physically or emotionally—slip a rope around Margaux's neck and slowly strangle her to death. It would be like imagining that Gandhi was a secret assassin. If we could cast doubt on Spiker's alibi, we'd be home free.

Although everyone on the jury had read about Spiker's scam, we wanted to give them a refresher course on what he'd tried to do.

Jen stood. "We call Julie Quinn to the stand."

Julie Quinn was *The New York Times* investigative journalist who had reported extensively on both the VW "Dieselgate" scandal and the Vanovax vaccine scam. Ms. Quinn was forty-six with a pleasant face unadorned by makeup. She wore glasses that had gone out of style, and her wavy brown hair was neatly combed. Her tan pantsuit was conservative.

"Ms. Quinn," Jen said, "can you first give us a short rundown of the Volkswagen emissions scandal of 2015?"

Slater stood, looking confused. "Your Honor, I object on the grounds of relevance. What's going on here?"

"Ms. Shek?"

"Your Honor, this will be short, and the relevance quickly apparent."

"Overruled."

Quinn looked at the judge. "The two scams—Dieselgate and Coronagate—are extraordinarily similar." She turned back to Jen. "In 2014, a man tested the emissions of a VW Jetta while driving. He found that the emissions were twenty-five times higher than the results during the EPA tests. It turned out that engineers in the company had rigged a device that detected when an emissions test was being conducted and altered the machinery so the vehicle would pass the test."

"And why is that similar to the scandal that's come to be called 'Coronagate'?"

"As the vaccine, one of many being developed for COVID-19, was nearing the production phase, Dr. Spiker found a problem that would make profitable manufacture of the drug impossible. He realized that the company would have to scrap the whole thing and lose an insane amount of money. Spiker would lose his job. It was the same situation the VW engineers found themselves in, and he solved it the same way. He designed a fake vaccine that would fool the FDA's spot tests."

"Would that vaccine protect anyone from COVID?"

"Not at all." Quinn shook her head. "The beauty of it was that no vaccine is one hundred percent effective, so the scam might have gone undiscovered. People would die."

"Were others aware of this scheme?"

"Yes, unbelievably. As with the VW scam, others knew what was going on and didn't speak up."

Jen asked, "Did Dr. Toll go along with the deception?"

"He did not, as suggested by the letter he gave to Mr. Goodlove. He was in a different department, by the way."

"What about Ms. Marchand?"

"According to that letter, she was also suspicious of Dr. Spiker."

"Do you think Dr. Spiker wanted to prevent Marchand and Toll from reveal—"

"Objection. Come on! Calls for speculation."

"Sustained." Judge Love glared at Jen then me.

"Psst." I got Jen's attention, and she came over to me and leaned down.

I whispered, "Ask her who else was in on it."

"She doesn't know."

"Ask her anyway."

Jen went back to the lectern. "Who else was in on this scam?"

Quinn said, "Nobody knows, and the investigation is ongoing, but my research suggests there are several unindicted coconspirators. I know it sounds unbelievable that anyone would go along with it, but the same could be said of Dieselgate."

The judge sustained Slater's objection to that answer.

Jen looked at me, and I discreetly chopped my right hand into the palm of the left—the ASL sign for stop.

"I have no more questions," she said.

Slater declined to cross-examine the witness.

We had successfully introduced the bogeyman to our jurors, and in one day, they'd get to meet the son of a bitch. In addition, Quinn's last answer suggested that even if Spiker didn't kill Margaux, there were others who shared Spiker's motive. Reasonable doubt.

Across the street from Odessa Orlano's Airbnb, Louella sat in her drab Ford Taurus—in the passenger seat. The older car was so nondescript it was almost invisible. Sitting in the passenger seat suggested she was waiting for someone, not running a stakeout. She smiled, thinking about all the little tricks of the trade rattling around in her head.

Orlano, Henry Spiker's alibi, apparently thought she could hide out in an undisclosed location to avoid unwanted attention, but Garrett's hacking consultant had had no trouble uncovering the address. The Airbnb was as cheap as they come. In one picture of the interior, the bed wasn't made.

It was seven a.m. on a rainy trash day. She'd figured that Odessa's husband would be the one to take the trash can to the street, and she smiled when the man opened the side door of the rental. After looking around, he ducked back in then reappeared wearing a rain jacket and holding a trash bag. While he put the bulging bag in the outside garbage can and started rolling it down the gravel driveway, Louella took a final puff and pushed her door open.

He glanced at her a few times, and the two came together on the street.

He looked at her from beneath his Seattle Sombrero rain hat. "You a reporter?"

"Mr. Orlano, I'm—"

"Oh, I know who you are." He positioned the trash can by the curb. "You're the private detective who interviewed Odessa."

Louella put her PI license back in her purse. "I was watching you when Odessa testified."

"So?" He put an elbow on the trash can, trying to act nonchalant. But the top of the can was too low, and he had to bend down, spoiling the effect.

Louella spared him embarrassment by looking away, pretending she hadn't noticed. "I saw the look in your eyes when Jen Shek mentioned perjury. Four years in a state pen. If you were involved—"

"I'm not. I ..."

Louella waited.

Mr. Orlano looked up at the house. "Let's go for a walk."

"We can talk in my car."

He looked at the house again. "No, let's go around the block."

They started walking, neither saying anything.

Louella broke the silence. "I can guarantee you she'll get busted. I might be able to help you limit the damage."

"How?"

"If she recants on the stand and throws herself on the mercy of the court, I'll make sure she's represented by Goodlove and Shek. No promises, but I'll bet he can keep her out of jail."

"Spiker didn't do it, you know."

Yeah, right. "You know that?"

"He just had too much on his plate, what with the FBI investigation. He wanted this thing put behind him."

"Why did your wife first lie and say she wasn't with him?"

Orlano was silent, obviously weighing things in his mind.

"I'm trying to help you here," Louella said.

The man thought for a while then took a deep breath and looked Louella in the eyes. "What did you ask, again?"

"Why did your wife first lie and then change her story?"

He huffed out a laugh. "That was Spiker's idea. He's a smart man, remember. He figured that if she first lied and then admitted it, the alibi would be more believable."

They walked in silence for a while. One woman brought her trash can to the street, wearing only pajamas and a hoodie. A big man walking a tiny dog nodded to them as he passed.

In response to a gust, Orlano tightened the chin strap on his hat. "Odessa won't admit the lie."

"She stubborn?"

"You don't know the half of it. I've been arguing with her. She says if she doesn't admit it, no one can prove it."

"What if she thought they'd put you on the stand?" Louella pulled her vape pen from the pocket of her slicker.

"Spiker says that the lawyers probably didn't put me on the list of witnesses, so it would be too late to call me."

"He's wrong. You'd be what's called a 'rebuttal witness.'" That wasn't a sure thing. Garrett said that sometimes a judge won't allow a rebuttal witness.

"But a husband can't testify against his wife, right?"

"He can't be forced to, but he can if he chooses to."

"Well," he said, "I won't do that. It would be the end of our marriage. And she'd go to jail."

"You want to stay married to a woman who pretended she had an affair? Was it for money?"

"Twenty thousand. We're in debt."

"Wouldn't you be better off free of her?"

Orlano sighed. "I've tried to leave her. I think she can change. It sounds corny, but I love her."

"Okay, here's a plan. You tell her that if she comes clean on the stand, the court will go easy on her, and Goodlove and Shek will represent her for free. Then tell her that you might be forced to testify as a rebuttal witness. Tell her that you won't commit perjury for her."

Orlano rubbed his eyes. "Let me think about it."

I watched Henry Spiker come into the courtroom and walk up the aisle.

No! Gone was the scary-looking Goth creep with stringy black hair and dark eye shadow. His neck looked sunburned where he'd had tattoos removed, and his long-sleeved shirt hid his arm tats. His hair was short with a few stylishly errant locks above his forehead. He wore a flannel shirt that I recognized from the Lands' End catalog with two buttons undone at the top, showing a white undershirt. If he'd been cast as the wholesome, friendly neighbor in a TV show, hair, makeup, and wardrobe couldn't have done a better job. He wore bellbottoms, effectively hiding his ankle monitor.

"Dr. Spiker," I said, "can you tell us about the vaccine you planned to produce that would not have protected anyone from COVID-19?"

"I can't." The nice-neighbor scenario fit even better when he started talking. He was convincingly mild. He produced an exaggerated sigh. "I'm under investigation, and I'm prohibited from talking about it." He looked at the jury. "But know that I deeply regret my actions. I got caught up in my pursuit of producing a vaccine that would make a difference, and when we were almost done, and we discovered that it wasn't feasible, I ... well, I made a mistake. A terrible mistake, and there's no excuse for it. I wish I could go back in time."

I leaned over so I could see his eyes. Yes, they were glistening. *Sheesh.* Worse, the jury seemed to be accepting it. Not eating it up, exactly, but only one juror, the anti-vaxxer, was rolling her eyes. The worst part was that I had been sure his testimony would be a win for our side. We all did. I decided to get out as quickly as I could.

I got Judge Love to declare him a hostile witness, which would let me ask leading questions, and started on his liaison with Orlano. If I could get details into the record, exposing him would be more dramatic.

"Is it true that you had an affair with a married woman, a Ms. Orlano?"

"Well," he said, "in this case, that wasn't a lapse in judgment on my part because I didn't know she was married. I never, *never* would have done that if I'd known. I thought it was completely innocent. And it was just the one day. The day that Ms. … uh … Marchand was killed."

"You drove down to Willits, why?"

"Ms. Orlano wanted to go there."

"Because it's such a romantic hotspot?"

"Objection. Prejudicial."

"Sustained."

"Did you choose a faraway location because it would give you an alibi for the entire day?"

"Ms. Orlano wanted to go there. I was lucky."

"You were lucky?" I asked.

"I was lucky because otherwise, people would think I killed Ms. Marchand."

"You didn't buy any gas on the trip?"

"We did, but it was a small station, and Ms. Orlano paid cash."

"You didn't buy anything, stay at a hotel? Nothing objective that would prove your alibi?"

Spiker actually managed to blush. "We drove to the Ohl Redwood Grove Park and went to a secluded spot. Laid out a blanket."

"We have lots of redwoods here."

"Ms. Orlano liked that place."

"Did you pay Ms. Orlano to provide you with an alibi?"

He clenched his teeth and leaned into the microphone. "Of course not. She didn't even want to admit it at first. That's when I learned she was married. If I'd known, I wouldn't have told the police about my alibi."

I looked down and shook my head. "No further questions."

In Slater's cross, he helped Spiker emphasize his remorse over the vaccine scam. It backfired somewhat because it mostly called attention to the enormity of his crime.

The day after Louella discovered the receipt, she walked into the AutoZone store on Fortuna Boulevard. She looked up at the ceiling. *Well, that sure warms my heart.* Several security cameras covered the entrance as well as the register. It was a long shot, but she wanted to confirm that Arthur had bought something at the store and find out what it was. Arthur's absence had been discovered the Monday after Margaux's murder. Had he really been only thirty miles away?

The big man behind the counter looked like a trucker, with full sleeve and neck tattoos.

"Whatcha lookin' for?" he asked.

Louella showed him her PI license. "I'm working on a murder case." That usually got people's attention. "How far back do your security cam files go?" Louella pointed to the cameras.

"We keep them for four months," he said.

Damn.

"What's the date you're looking for?"

"May eleventh of this year."

"Eight twelve in the morning?"

Louella squinted.

"Total of $187.52?"

Louella looked at the copy of the receipt. "That's right, Rain Man. What, are you some kind of savant? How did you—"

He laughed. "The police are months ahead of you."

"Meaning?"

"They arrested that punk, thanks to yours truly." He banged his chest with a fist like a one-armed gorilla.

Louella pulled a stool from a nearby register and sat. "You want to start from the beginning?" *He can't wait to tell his story.*

"You betcha. So, this punk teenager comes in. He buys a slim jim—the tool for opening a locked car door, not the jerky—and a dent puller set. He bought some other random things for camouflage, but of course I knew he was looking to steal an older model car, one that those tools would work on. Lot of those around here."

The man paused, enjoying his storytelling. "So I watch him drive away—"

"He already had a car?"

"Yeah. A Honda Civic, but I didn't see the plate. I still knew he was planning to steal another car or something. I called the cops. They caught him the next day. They were on the lookout, and they found him checking out parked cars. He had the burglary tools on him. Turns out the credit card he used was stolen, and he had a rap sheet longer than my dick."

"Was he convicted?"

"Sure was. Name of Petey Ketch. He's currently a guest of the Humboldt County Correctional Facility."

Louella thanked him and dropped two twenties on the counter.

"What's this for?"

"That's what I would have given you to convince you to talk."

He laughed. "Only forty bucks?"

Louella peeled off another twenty. "Thanks, buddy."

Chapter Twenty-Three

THE DAY AFTER SPIKER testified, it was time for our big coup: demonstrating that his alibi was fake.

The night before, Jen, Nicole, and I had our screen tests. We needed to determine which of us could most effectively convey relief. My wife and daughter both laughed at me when I looked skyward and mouthed, "Thank you!"

"Hey, I was just joking." I tried again, just taking a deep breath, followed by a slow smile. I kept it subtle. Jen gave me a six, Nicole, a seven.

Jen scored below me. She's better at being inscrutable than wearing her emotions on her sleeve. Nicole won the contest—her nod and satisfied smile best conveyed relief. She would perform the direct examination of Ms. Orlano.

After getting Orlano declared a hostile witness, Nicole led her through her alleged day with Spiker. The details matched well except for a few things that anyone with an imperfect memory might misremember.

"Isn't it strange, Ms. Orlano, that you two didn't happen to stop anywhere with a security camera?"

She shrugged. "I don't think so."

Nicole kept an eye on her watch and got the timing just right. "Isn't it true, Ms. Orlano, that Henry Spiker paid you twenty thousand dollars to make up his alibi?" At that exact moment, Orlano's husband walked up the aisle.

"No," Orlano said. "Of course not." Her voice trembled. The mention of the precise amount had to have spooked her. *C'mon, cave!*

"Dr. Spiker asked you to first lie about the affair then admit it, so as to make the alibi seem more believa— Just a second, please." Nicole went to the rail, and Orlano's husband whispered something in her ear. He probably said, "I'm whispering in your ear now."

Nicole took a clipboard from the defense table and handed it to him. He signed a random sheet of paper as planned.

She turned back to let Odessa see her nod and her satisfied smile. "I apologize for that. Dr. Spiker asked you to first lie about the affair then admit it, to make the alibi seem more believable. Is that right?"

A sheen of sweat appeared on Odessa's forehead. "No. That's ridiculous."

"If I call your husband to the stand as a rebuttal witness, will he corroborate your made-up story?"

"Objection." Slater stood. "I don't know what game they're playing, but Ms. Goodlove is clearly badgering the witness."

"Your Honor, it's a reasonable question." Nicole's tone was confident, not strident.

"Overruled."

Nicole looked Odessa in the eyes. "Will he corroborate your story?"

There was a second of fear in the witness's eyes, then it changed to relief. Not feigned relief like ours, but the genuine article. Perhaps Spiker had warned her we might try some tricks, or she'd watched a lot of TV legal dramas, but however it happened, Odessa had figured out we were bluffing.

She leaned forward. "Of course he'll corroborate it because it's the *truth*. He's forgiven me for my indiscretion, and he knows I'm sorry. It happened just like I said, but it was just a physical thing, and I'll never do it again. But it's between my husband and me."

Damn! I wanted to bury my head in my hands, but that wouldn't look good in front of the jury.

Only five hours after learning the name of the man who had, in all probability, driven Arthur's car into the river, Louella found herself sitting across from him—Mr. Petey Ketch—in the Humboldt jail visiting area.

The kid was nineteen, thin, and feminine looking with a narrow face and a sullen look. His hair was blond, and his lips seemed unusually red. Louella looked closely. *No, not lipstick.*

"I got some bad news for you, kid," Louella said.

He frowned. "Who are you?"

"We found the car you dumped in the river."

"Bullshit."

"White 2019 Honda Civic. Ring a bell?"

His eyebrows jumped, just a little. Enough to signal that a gong had indeed gone off in his head.

"Here's the deal, Petey. I don't care about you. I don't care about your crimes. Whether you rot in jail or get out tomorrow means nothing to me. I just want to know one thing: where you got that car. That's it. Tell me that, and I'll put in a good word with the prosecutor. I'll also send you a check for a thousand dollars."

They went back and forth a bit, and eventually Louella convinced him to talk.

He nodded. "Okay. Here's the story. I didn't steal it."

"I'm outta here." She stood. "Good luck, kid."

"No, wait," he said. "I kinda didn't steal it. Somebody wanted me to take it."

Louella said nothing.

"I was in the parking lot of the Antioch BART station." BART was the subway system down in San Francisco. "So I'm walking along, minding my own business, and I see the car."

"Monday, May tenth?"

"Yeah. So the window was open and, get this, the keys were on the dashboard. I'd have been an idiot not to take it."

That's debatable. "Why did you drive up here, and why did you dump it?"

"I thought you only wanted to know where I got it."

Louella said, "A thousand is a lot of money."

He shrugged. "I was going to a friend's house in Crescent City. After a while, I got to thinking about why someone would make a car so easy to steal. I'd read about bait bikes, where they put a GPS transmitter thing in the bike, and they use it to catch the thief. So I thought maybe that's what was going on with this car. I started getting nervous, and so I figured I'd drive it into a lake or something so it couldn't transmit the GPS anymore."

"So you bought tools to steal another car then drove the Honda Civic into the river."

He looked down at his hands.

"The police already know about the tools, dumbass. That's why you were picked up."

"Yeah, that's what happened."

"Did you take anything from the car?" Louella asked. "Like a notebook?"

"No way. Nothing."

"Thanks, kid." Louella got up. "I'll mail you your check. I'll include the name of a good lawyer and put in a word for you with the DA."

Usually by the time closing arguments roll around, I have a good feeling for whether we'd prevail. I'd also know if my client was guilty. Those two things were not true in Arthur's case. I knew that Arthur's car had driven both to and from the area of the killing. That was pretty damning evidence.

The prosecution went first. Derek Slater stood at the lectern looking down at his notes, immobile, letting the tension build up. He slowly raised his gaze to the jurors.

"Amnesia," he said.

I gave Jen a private eye roll. *Was the jury buying the drama?*

"What a convenient thing," he continued. "The detectives can question you all they want, but they always … get the same answer: *I. Don't. Remember.* Where were you on the afternoon of May the ninth? I don't remember. Did you put a rope around Margaux

Marchand's neck and strangle her? Sorry, I don't remember."

Slater held his hand out toward our team. "The defense presented an expert who said the amnesia is real. She showed us brain scans and was pretty convincing. Maybe the defendant does have amnesia. But you know what? It doesn't matter if he's faking or not; either way, there's no point in questioning him. Luckily, we don't need to because we have all the evidence necessary to tell us that Arthur took Margaux for a picnic, snuck up behind her, put a rope around her neck, strangled her, and fled.

"How do we know he took her on a picnic? His car shows up on the gas station's security camera traveling south after she was killed. 'But not north before the killing!' the defense yells. 'Must be someone else's car,' they say. Well, maybe the car did go north, and we just didn't see it. Maybe it was passing—"

"Objection!" Jen, Nicole, and I all jumped up and yelled the word simultaneously.

The judge jumped back and grabbed her heart. It took her ten seconds to recover. "What the hell—heck is this? If this is some kind of a joke or some stunt you put together, Goodlove—"

"Approach, Your Honor?"

Up at the bench, I said, "Mr. Slater is attempting to introduce new evidence."

The picture of innocence, Slater held his arms in front of him as if surrendering. "Not at all. I'm just proposing a hypothetical."

"My chambers. Now."

Jen, Slater, and I followed the judge. She was clearly frailer than she had been at the first bail hearing back in June.

Boxes were stacked in one corner of Judge Love's chambers, and most of the photos and paintings had been removed from the wall. She was preparing to die.

Once we were settled, Slater described the evidence that Arthur's car had been invisible going north because it was passing a truck. He showed her the footage.

"The timing of that," Slater said, "exactly matches the GPS track from Marchand's phone. There's no question that Arthur's car is on the other side of that truck."

"And you didn't discover that until after you rested your case?" the judge asked.

"Correct. But of course, I wasn't going to present the evidence in my closing statement."

"What is it you were going to say?"

"Simply this: Maybe Arthur's car was passing a truck when it went by the gas station or wasn't seen for some other reason."

The judge looked at me. "That sounds reasonable, doesn't it?"

We went back and forth, but it wasn't an argument we could win. Judge Love ruled that Slater could mention the possibility the car was passing the truck. Anything more, and she'd declare a mistrial. Which would be a win for Slater, of course. She warned him of the consequences if he deliberately tried to trigger one.

Back in court, Slater rewound his brain to the paragraph that had been interrupted, went through it, and continued with, "Well, maybe the car did go north, and we just didn't see it. Maybe it was passing a big semitruck when it drove by the security camera. Who knows? But there's one thing we do know. Arthur's DNA was on the murder weapon. When he pulled the rope tight, some of his skin cells were deposited on it.

"The defense wants you to think that Henry Spiker killed Ms. Marchand, but *his* DNA wasn't found on the rope. *His* car wasn't seen driving to or from the murder scene. And finally, Spiker has an alibi. He was way down in Willits on that day, so he couldn't have been north of Orick."

He paused then chuckled. "I'm sorry, I shouldn't laugh about mental illness, but the teenage witness who said he saw the defendant in Loleta? Even the voices in his head told him he was imagining it."

Slater went on, summarizing his chronology of the crime with evidence to support each point in the timeline. It was depressing. I closed my eyes and followed Toby's advice: no fortune-telling! Don't foresee Slater winning and sending the meek Arthur Toll to prison.

My turn. At the lectern, I, like Slater, let the suspense build. The clock ticked, and the scent of my own perspiration reached my nose.

"It's a pretty simple story, actually," I said. "Dr. Henry Spiker came up with a scheme that would make his fortune yet kill thousands of innocent people. Even he doesn't deny that. Can you imagine anything more evil?" I let that sink in. "To prevent his scam from being uncovered, he killed Ms. Margaux Marchand and injected Arthur with a drug he knew would wipe Arthur's memory. Mr. Slater says that Dr. Spiker has an alibi. C'mon. Did you see the fear in Ms. Orlano's eyes when Ms. Shek mentioned the penalty for perjury? And in this day and age, with Google Timeline, security cameras, and credit card receipts, how could two people drive to and spend a day in a faraway town and not leave a trace?"

I shrugged. "But okay. Okay, let's say that you believe his alibi. Dr. Spiker is rich. He could have hired a man to kill the woman who suspected his misdeeds. Or someone else could have killed her. Her husband? The mystery man who fathered her unborn child, who has never been found? An unindicted coconspirator in Spiker's scam? An animal rights activist who objects to the torturing of animals in the labs? There's plenty of reasonable doubt in this case."

After a pause. "The prosecution has shown a video of one of the most common cars in the country traveling south after the murder. Could be anybody. They want you to believe that somehow Arthur's car snuck past the security camera going north, as if it had Harry Potter's invisibility cloak or something." I scoffed. *Yeah, I'm going to go to hell.*

"And finally, let's not forget the letter that Arthur gave me. In it, he explained how he and Margaux were suspicious of Dr. Spiker and how they were investigating him. He'd written, 'To be opened upon the event that something happens to me' on the outside of the envelope. He was in fear of his life and that of Ms. Marchand. Nine days later, she was murdered, and Arthur was almost certainly injected with a drug that cruelly took away his entire life. That letter, ladies and gentlemen, clearly tells us who murdered Margaux Marchand."

Chapter Twenty-Four

I COULDN'T UNDERSTAND WHAT was taking the jury so long. It wasn't that complicated a case, was it? Maybe it seemed simple to me because I'd spent so many hours going over it.

The closing arguments were on a Thursday, and on the following Wednesday, we finally got word that they'd reached a verdict.

I hated looking at jurors' faces when they file into court. Were they smiling? Did they look at the defendant? To avoid speculating, I put my chin against my chest and closed my eyes. The only sound was that of twenty-four feet walking in from the deliberation room.

It was at that moment a revelation popped into my consciousness. *I know where Arthur's lab notebook is!* Well, I didn't know for sure, but I had a pretty good idea based on what Louella had reported about Arthur's car. It was too late to influence the verdict, but if Arthur was convicted, it might provide exculpatory evidence that could get him a new trial. I was so engaged in my thoughts about how to retrieve it and what it might tell us that I almost missed the verdict.

Jen nudged me from my reverie. I opened my eyes. The jury foreman was standing.

"We, the jury in the above-entitled action, find the defendant, Arthur Dickens Toll, not guilty of the crime of first-degree murder in violation of Penal Code one eight seven …"

I almost didn't believe it. Arthur's nightmare was over. He hugged each of us in turn, tears in his eyes. Arthur had a whole new life to look forward to. Literally, since his old life had been taken from him.

The day after the verdict, Louella and I found ourselves on a tiny jet, flying down to San Francisco. It was a long shot, but I reasoned that if Arthur had abandoned his car at a BART station, he'd probably taken a train. Perhaps he had his lab notebook with him, and he'd left it behind when he lost his memory. *Definitely a long shot.*

"So this is just to satisfy your overactive curiosity, right, boss?" she said.

I had to raise my voice to be heard over the thrumming engine. "Tell me you don't want to see it. See the last entry."

"What is it you think he's going to write? 'Dear Diary, today I didn't kill Margaux'?"

"You've seen his earlier lab notebooks, right?"

"Yeah." Louella looked down at the coast.

"Well, you saw how he detailed everything in his life. He was positively anal about it. There might something that enlightens us."

"But if Spiker injected him, as you suggested, he can't have written about that."

I shrugged. "Maybe the drug took a while to take effect."

Louella took the pack of pretzels from the stewardess. "We'll know soon enough—if we find it."

"Did you ever find out who broke into your house and threatened you?"

"Nope. My guess is Spiker hired him, but we'll never know. By the way, looks like we'll never find the father of Margaux's unborn child, either."

The man at the BART lost and found department was roly, poly, and jolly. He was bald with a dark red beard. "Welcome to BART's lost and found. You lose it, we find it."

I wondered how many times he'd made that joke. It didn't really make sense.

He loved his job and loved talking about it. "My biggest joy is reuniting things with their owners. You should see their faces. Can I tell you some of the things I've found?"

"Well, right now, we're looking for a notebook that looks like this." I'd purchased a notebook of the same type that Arthur used. I held it up.

The fat man took it then gave it back. "Nice leather. Sure. Follow me. Did you know we get about forty pounds of keys every month? We've found wheelchairs, rollerblades, a piñata with Goofy on it. After ninety days, everything goes to charity."

Louella and I exchanged a look. *Damn!* It had been five months since Arthur's car had been stolen from the Antioch BART station.

"But we're way, way behind. When was the notebook lost?"

"Last May," I said.

"Okay. Maybe."

Louella and I dug through the two bins holding the oldest books.

I yelled, "Eureka!" when I found it. I showed it to Louella, and she gave me a thumbs up.

We wasted no time. On a bench outside the office, I flipped to the last entry, and we read it silently together.

I put my finger on one paragraph and asked, "Date rape drug?"

She nodded. "Probably."

We finished reading, and I closed the book. "Well, that certainly presents me with a dilemma."

Chapter Twenty-Five

BACK IN MY OFFICE, with Louella standing by the window drinking coffee and a fire in the fireplace, I reread Arthur's final entry in his lab notebook.

May 10, 2021. This entry will be the last in my lab notebook. Perhaps no one will ever read it, yet it is my avowed habit to record everything important in my life.

Yesterday, I killed Margaux Marchand.

It may be deemed an accidental killing, caused in no small part by her stubbornness and the strength of her talent for persuasion. Yet the majority of the blame falls on me because of the flaw in my character, the fatal flaw of meekness, which enabled her to persuade me to perform the despicable act which ran contrary to my better judgment and which led to her untimely death.

Although we'd spent much time together in the laboratory, and it was in her nature to flirt, I had studiously avoided any conduct of a sexual nature. I admit to an attraction in that regard, but our workplace relationship rendered any such behavior inappropriate however much I might have wished for it. Ever since the day I watched her run naked in the surf, I found it most difficult to suppress thoughts of that nature.

On the morning of Sunday, May 9, 2021, Margaux persuaded me to take her on a picnic, the destination of which she held in confidence. I assented only after receiving her grave assurances that the event would be totally platonic in both essence and fact. I picked her up, and she directed me to the Lost Man Creek Trail north of Orick. She had prepared a picnic lunch, and with the victuals stored securely in her rucksack, we proceeded up the trail.

After a vigorous hike, during which I kept pace with her only through a considerable exertion, she turned off into the forest. I saw no trail and objected, asking why we shouldn't consume our lunch beside the path. She expostulated, with surprising vehemence, that we could better enjoy the ambiance of the forest when out of sight of the manmade footpath. "Trust me," she said.

I followed her, and true to her prediction, we came upon an enchanting clearing where the redwood needles lay like a blanket on the forest floor. She unpacked the lunch, which included a bottle of French wine and a container of expensive foie gras. The meal was indeed succulent to a degree I had never experienced, and, as she'd predicted, the natural environment, free of any evidence of man, accentuated the pleasure. Thinking back, she drank very little wine. In any case, true to her vow, she made no sexual advances and refrained from the flirting in which she often engaged at the lab.

After our repast, I felt an unusual degree of inebriation, of a level unexpected even with my consumption of wine. I went into the forest to relieve myself, careful not to proceed so far that I might lose my way.

When I returned, I discovered Margaux totally naked, lying in a seductive pose on the bed of brown pine and redwood needles. I backed away, shaking my head, but she popped up, took my hands, and pulled me into a close embrace. I cannot overstate the power of her sumptuous, curvaceous body against mine. She crushed her breasts against my chest and rubbed her lower body lasciviously upon my groin.

She pulled me down with her, and any resolve I had to that point fled. The totality of my capitulation still amazes me. I resigned myself to the upcoming single act of sexual intercourse, to be followed by an injunction that the inappropriate behavior never be repeated. Would that I had known the sequelae of her request, I'd have severed the chains of my desire and taken flight. But I felt a strange compulsion to surrender to her demands.

She whispered that she didn't desire copulation but only manual stimulation. At that point, she pulled a length of nylon rope and an electronic device, which I recognized as a pulse oximeter, from her backpack. She whispered in my ear that I was to put the rope around her neck and twist it so that the resulting anoxia would bring her to fainting just at the moment of orgasm.

I objected strenuously but again found an incomprehensible inability to resist. I had heard of erotic asphyxiation and understood that it greatly enhanced the intensity of orgasm but never thought I would encounter someone who would wish to engage in that risky behavior.

"But this could kill you," said I.

She assured me that by using the pulse oximeter, we would avoid all risk. She instructed me that if her oxygen saturation should fall below 78%, I was to release the pressure on the rope until the reading rose to 85%, at which point I should resume twisting the rope. I inferred that she had empirically determined those values from past experience. Under no circumstances was I to stop until she achieved orgasm.

What happened next, I cannot say, but can only deduce. I came to my senses lying next to her dead body, the rope still clutched in my hand. Whether the pulse oximeter failed to protect her or my inexplicable level of inebriation precluded my attention to the levels, I cannot say. It may also have been that my extreme level of sexual arousal played a role.

In a haze, I ran from the scene, crashing through the forest until I came upon the Lost Man Creek Trail. I have no recollection of driving to my home, but I must have since I woke in my bed the next morning, drenched in sweat and with a prodigious fever. My car was in front of my house, haphazardly parked.

I had no doubts of the veracity of what I'd experienced, to wit, that I'd killed a human being as a result of my poor decisions and, of more importance, my flaws of character. Besides the legal peril, which would certainly lead to a long period of incarceration, it was a memory with which I could not live. Decades of existence with the image of her dead, naked body on the forest floor haunting me was something I was unwilling to accept, but suicide was strictly forbidden by the Christian tenets I'd vowed to uphold.

It was only after hours of contemplation, my head in my hands, that my mind fastened on the obvious solution. I drove to my bank and emptied the contents of my local checking account. After a hurried trip to the lab, I gathered the necessary materials, drove down to Antioch, and parked my car at the BART station. I left the window open and the keys on the dashboard.

It is on a BART train that I am writing this final entry in my lab notebook, with what goal I am unsure. It may be because of my vow to record everything, or perhaps I just need to get this terrible episode off my chest. Before it's too late.

My plan is to get off the train in San Francisco, walk to a disreputable area of town, keep my cash but discard my wallet, and inject myself with a dose of propolofan sufficient to induce total, irreversible amnesia. In that way, Arthur Toll will cease to exist, yet I will avoid committing the mortal sin of taking my own life.

May God have mercy on my soul.

Arthur Dickens Toll

"So," I said, "we have a dilemma."

Louella came over and sat. "To tell Arthur or not."

"Part of me wants to put this whole notebook in the fire."

"But there's information in there that could help Arthur learn about his life. Plus, important data from his research. Actually, it's relevant to his research."

I nodded. "True. By having erased the traumatic experience from his memory, he avoids the depression that it might have caused."

I opened the center drawer of my desk and fished out a box cutter. I cut out the two incriminating pages as close to the binding as possible. I handed the book to Louella. "Do you think he'd notice?"

She leafed through it, spreading apart the pages before and after the ones I removed. "He might. If so, you can just shrug and act puzzled."

I looked at the fire again and considered the remote possibility that someone else could be charged with

Margaux's murder. I folded the excised pages and put them in an envelope and labeled it. I opened the office safe that had once held Arthur's letter, placed the envelope in it, and locked it.

I invited Nicole and Carly over for dinner but made sure my daughter arrived first. I couldn't share the discovery with my sister.

Sitting around the dining room, breathing in the delicious aroma of baking lasagna, I said, "Louella and I found Arthur's last lab notebook, and he'd written down everything that happened when Margaux died."

Jen gasped.

Nicole asked, "Would it have helped the defense?"

"No. And now I know what happened."

They waited. Nicole rolled her hand impatiently.

"He killed her," I said, "but it was mostly an accident."

Jen frowned. "Mostly?"

"Out in the woods, during a picnic, I think Margaux slipped Arthur a date rape drug. But what is clear is that she induced Arthur to help her with erotic asphyxiation by choking her with a rope while stimulating her. Things went too far, and she died."

I answered a few questions and described Arthur's actions following her death.

Jen said, "So it was all a big coincidence. Arthur gave you a letter asking us to investigate if something happened to him, and something did happen to him, but—"

"But what happened was totally unrelated to Spiker and the vaccine department."

"Exactly." Jen nodded.

We sat in silence until the doorbell rang. When I opened it, Carly signed, "What's the big occasion?"

"Occasion?"

"From your email, it sounded like you wanted to show me something."

I can never hide anything from her twin sense. "Well, it is a big occasion, in a way." I called Jen and Nicole into the living room, went to a closet, and pulled out two brown paper packages.

"I had these photographs framed, and unless any of you object"—my voice got a little husky—"I'm going to hang them here in the living room."

The three people I love most in the world sent me puzzled looks.

I unwrapped the first photo and hung it up. It was a snapshot I'd taken, and it showed Raquel, my first wife, moments after she'd given birth to Toby. Her beauty came through even though she'd just gone through a long, difficult labor. Her dark hair was disheveled and soaked with sweat, but she wore a wide smile as she held our newborn son against her breast.

"Oh, Dad, that's a wonderful picture." Nicole's eyes brimmed with tears. "I'd forgotten about it."

I unwrapped the second photo and hung it next to the first. It showed Toby holding his cousin, Patricia, just days before she'd died on the operating table while getting a cochlear implant. He was seventeen, and she was one and a half. She had her arms around his neck and her cheek pressed against his scraggly beard. Their smiles matched the one in the photo of Raquel.

Carly's eyes also filled with tears, something that rarely happens. One spilled down her cheek. She hugged me then stood back. "I'm okay with those photos, but what about you, bro?"

I pointed to my chest and slid my hand down then put four fingers of my right hand against my chin and pulled them away into the palm of my left: *I'm good.*

Acknowledgments

I'm so grateful for the help I've had with this book.

I had a great beta reader crew, as usual. Thanks to my wonderful wife, Lena, who is always the first reader of my books. My writing buddy, Allison Maruska (author of the bestseller, *The Fourth Descendant*), helped me discover many important problems with my first draft.

Thanks as well to Gail Summerville, Linda Johnson, Nicholas Hoyle, Bruce Lutz, Rigby Taylor, Charlie Miess, Andrea Porter, Les Tucker, Bruce Kunkle, John Lawton, and others.

My copy editor, Julie MacKenzie from FreeRangeEditorial.com, finds way too many errors but is still a pleasure to work with.

My audiobook producer/narrator, Nick Sullivan (NickSullivan.net) is a genius and brings my books to life. I'm lucky to have found him.

Also by Al Macy

Becoming a Great Sight-Reader—or Not! Learn from my Quest for Piano Sight-Reading Nirvana
Drive, Ride, Repeat: The Mostly True Account of a Cross-Country Car and Bicycle Adventure

Contact Us: A Jake Corby Sci-Fi Thriller
The Antiterrorist: A Jake Corby Sci-Fi Thriller
The Universe Next Door: A Jake Corby Sci-Fi Thriller
The Christmas Planet and Other Stories

Yesterday's Thief: An Eric Beckman Paranormal Sci-Fi Thriller
Sanity's Thief: An Eric Beckman Paranormal Thriller
Democracy's Thief: An Eric Beckman Paranormal Thriller
A Mind Reader's Christmas: An Eric Beckman Mystery
The Day Before Yesterday's Thief: A Prequel to the Eric Beckman Series
The Mind Reader's Journey: An Eric Beckman Paranormal Thriller

The Protected Witness: An Alex Booker Thriller
The Abducted Heiress: An Alex Booker Thriller

Al Macy

* * *

Conclusive Evidence: A Novel
Sufficient Evidence: A Novel
Damaging Quarantine: A Short Story
Damaging Evidence: A Novel
Legal Lies: A Short Story

About the Author

Al Macy lives with his wife in the redwood forest of far Northern California. After earning a Bachelor's in Physiological Psychology from Cornell and a PhD in Neuroscience from the University of Michigan, he did brain research at UC Berkeley.

Next, he switched careers and wrote educational computer games. Then he founded and headed a small software company in the Bay Area. After retiring from that, he became a struggling jazz musician.

Finally, he started writing books and has found himself unable to stop.

Printed in Great Britain
by Amazon